Angel Blessings Imagine

Patty Callahan

BookLocker

Saint Petersburg, Florida

Dedication

This book is dedicated to angels everywhere—our Archangels, Guardian Angels, Earth Angels, Fur Angels, deceased loved ones, and to everyone who has love in their heart. We may not be able to see you, but we know you are here with us. *Believe! Imagine!*

Angel blessings to you all.

Table of Contents

Acknowledgments ix

Preface xi

Introduction... 1

Part I - Life Before 3

    Chapter 1 – No! 5

    Chapter 2 – Thirty Days of Hell....................................9

    Chapter 3 – Rejuvenation 15

    Chapter 4 – Memories...21

    Chapter 5 – Their Favorite Place 25

    Chapter 6 – From Paradise to the Library 31

    Chapter 7 – Library and Tapestry Rooms 35

    Chapter 8 – School of Wisdom 41

    Chapter 9 – A Word to the Wise.................................45

    Chapter 10 – Home Sweet Home 49

    Chapter 11 – Backyard Fairyland...............................55

    Chapter 12 – Old Friends 61

    Chapter 13 – Party Time with the Leprechauns,
       Fairies & Trees 67

Part II - New Worlds.. 73

    Chapter 14 – Under the Sea with Legna 75

    Chapter 15 – Bubble Magic 81

    Chapter 16 – Aquarium Auditorium...........................87

Chapter 17 – Ocean Depths: Featuring Archangel
Manakel 91

Chapter 18 – Stars Amid the Cosmos: Featuring
Archangel Orion... 97

Chapter 19 – Truth & Justice: Featuring Archangel
Mariel 103

Chapter 20 – On Board a UFO 109

Chapter 21 – First Look: Featuring Archangel Barachiel 115

Chapter 22 – The Miracle of Fire 123

Chapter 23 – Karma & The Wee Ones: Featuring
Archangels Nathaniel & Ariana 129

Chapter 24 – Trip to Somewhere............................ 135

Chapter 25 – The Crystal Residence...................... 139

Chapter 26 – Home and Garden............................. 145

Chapter 27 – Getting to Know Them 151

Part III · Lessons Learned 157

Chapter 28 – What Evil Lurks 159

Chapter 29 – Research at the School of Wisdom 169

Chapter 30 – Good vs Evil: Featuring Archangel Phanuel...177

Chapter 31 – The Miracle of Water: Featuring
Archangel Arariel 185

Chapter 32 – Sky and Stormy: Featuring Archangel
Gadiel 191

Chapter 33 – Shaken to the Core: Featuring Archangels
Gersisa, Christiel & Purlimiek 197

Chapter 34 – Calming Sandalwood: Featuring
    Archangel Fhelyai 203

Chapter 35 – Butterfly Fields.................................207

Chapter 36 – Inner Planet: Featuring the Return
    of Archangel Gersisa 213

Chapter 37 – Energy Center: Featuring Archangels
    Selaphiel & Butyalil...219

Part IV - Until We Meet Again 223

Chapter 38 – Archangel Council: Featuring 30
    Archangels 225

Chapter 39 – Glistening...231

Chapter 40 – Diamonds 237

Chapter 41 – We Did It 243

Chapter 42 – Reunion 249

Chapter 43 – Home at Last 253

Chapter 44 – Merriment..261

Afterward 267

Appendix I - Your Guide to the Angels....................269

Appendix II - Archangel Specialties 283

About the Author 297

Acknowledgments

Thank you to:

Archangel Gabriel for the morning messages

All the archangels, guardian angels, earth angels, spirit guides, and departed loved ones

My husband, sons, and brothers

My dear friends Janet and Sam

My cousins Kerryl, Donna, and Marilyn

Patty's mom, proofreader from the heavens

Mentor davidji, davidji.com

Mentor Mike Dooley, mikedooley.com

Mentor Angela Hoy, Booklocker, and all the contributors to Writer's Weekly, writersweekly.com, booklocker.com

Editor Rickey Pittman, the Bard of the South, who turned every correction into a learning, bardofthesouth.com

Angel Enthusiast Kyle Gray, kylegray.co.us

Angel Enthusiast Diana Cooper, dianacooper.com

Angel Enthusiast Lorna Byrne, lornabyrne.com

My followers, book buyers, and readers

—Angel blessings to you all

Preface

She's back. Our beloved Angie had countless adventures in *Angel Blessings Believe*, the first book in this series. She is like so many of us, full of love, always trying to do her best, looking for the good in all people and situations, and wanting the basics—clean air, water, and food. Angie enjoys flowers, butterflies, birds, shells, the beach, the woodlands, and all beautiful God-given nature, from the glorious sunrises and sunsets to the aurora borealis. She is upset with all those who rule with greed and upset when people hurt others.

When she first met the Archangels, she was overjoyed and came up with pet names for them—Raziel, her Rainbow Wizard; Haniel, her Moonbeam—Azrael, her Christmas Angel—to name a few. Her special invitation to an Angel Council left her speechless—well, almost. Angie is never at a loss for words.

A modest soul, she couldn't believe that she was chosen to save the loving souls on earth. She didn't think she was worthy. The love and caring in her heart, lifetime after lifetime, had moved her to the top of the list of candidates.

We grew to expect her to question everything, something many of us wouldn't dare to consider in the presence of supreme beings. We were the sideline cheerleaders observing her mission to save the loving souls. Her soulmate, Andrew, had traveled with Angie for lifetimes throughout eternity. You could feel their unbounded love at their first meeting after years apart. Mary and Matthew joined them to complete the foursome. Archangel Metatron suggested they incarnate as twins. Angie and Mary grew up together, while Andrew and Matthew also shared a twin life. We watched the inseparable foursome through their many adventures. The wedding of twins marrying twins was picture perfect.

We witnessed our dreams of hope for the future on the new earth come true. A Paradise we could envision for our planet right now—if only. If only people would rise in love, spread love to overcome the greed and selfishness that ruined the earth. If only the peacemakers would spread their love worldwide to give peace a chance.

If you have not read *Angie Blessings Believe*, we highly suggest that you add it to your reading list. Experiencing the love, caring, sharing, archangels, the hereafter, and the future are treasures you won't soon forget. If you have asked yourself, "What happens when we die?" this book is for you.

Introduction

Angie, Andrew, Mary, and Matthew had been tasked with a mission to save the loving souls on earth and relocate them to a duplicate but unspoiled earth. The new planet was Paradise in every sense imaginable. There were no hospitals because no one became sick. There were no police because everyone got along. No one went through the Veil of Forgetfulness. Souls remembered life on the astral plane and why they had decided to return to earth. Free will included loving choices, no more egos. Together they enjoyed a collective consciousness where they could read each other's minds. If someone needed help, they all knew to rush to their side.

Aliens from the far reaches of the universe had revealed themselves, as had the leprechauns, fairies, Tree People, and all the elementals who had previously remained hidden from view. There were all colors of people but no division. They enjoyed different dialects, but they communicated in the universal language of thought since they read each other's minds. Rainwater filled the reservoirs at night, and that water contained all the nutrients their bodies needed. Food was a delicacy and not a necessity. Transportation was through brainwaves or crystals, which also lit up their homes and communities. The Creator had thought of everything, and these loving souls deserved and enjoyed their new, pristine planet earth.

The negative souls who were not permitted to shift to the new earth had gone straight to the resting area on the astral plane. There they would stay and receive counseling until they repented and could be allowed to inhabit a planet. They would be banished to the farthest reaches of the universe to a primitive world with no conveniences. They would have to start over like the cavemen in history books. A tough life, to put it mildly. They would need to work off the negative karma that had turned their souls dark.

Come along and "imagine" the Archangels working with the planets throughout the galaxies. Enjoy getting reacquainted with the Archangels from Angle Blessings Believe. You will meet new Archangels, learn about their specialties, and recognize them by their distinctive colors. You will have a seat at the dawn of a primitive age. Follow the negative souls as they learn to live in caves for shelter and grow, hunt, and fish for their food. You will also travel to advanced, unique planets. Surrounded by angels, you will be able to do all this without leaving the comfort of your favorite chair. Join Angie, Andrew, Mary, and Matthew as their journey continues into the great unknown as you ask yourselves, "Is there anybody out there?"

Part I
Life Before

Chapter 1 – No!

NO!" Angie's emphatic proclamation reverberated throughout the collective minds of the Universe. The Creator, surrounded by the starlight of millions of souls, with the Archangels swirling around, took a momentary pause while everything shuttered. Even the farthest reaches of the Universe were shaken and alarmed, having no idea what had just happened.

"Already?" Angie protested. "How can any of these negative souls be ready to incarnate? They ruined an entire planet! They lied about polluted water and unbreathable air! Many harmed the very people they had taken an oath to protect!"

Michael did not expect this reaction from this tender soul with pure love in her heart. Archangels, who knew Angie well, materialized at Michael's side the moment the Universe trembled. Her close friends, her soul mates, witnessed Angie's reaction and were surprised into silence. This reaction was not typical for their calm, level-headed pal they knew so well. *Angie is known to question everything, but fury? She didn't have an angry bone in her body.* But right now, everyone everywhere froze in their tracks, spell-bound and afraid to breathe or move a muscle.

Using a very calm, patient approach, Michael explained, "Angie, it is not as bad as you are envisioning. We are not talking about allowing *all* the negative souls to incarnate, just the first wave. Those caught up in the negativity have expressed sorrow, have endured long resting periods and intense counseling sessions. More importantly, they are remorseful. It is time for them to move forward to commence the arduous task of repairing their karma. They know that it will take many lifetimes to undo the damage they have done to their souls."

"*Thirty days* to experience hell on earth doesn't seem to be enough compared to the damage they caused over many lifetimes! I don't understand how they can be ready to incarnate this soon," protested Angie.

Michael continued. "During 30-nightfalls, they had to live with undrinkable water, unbreathable air, poisoned food, disease-spreading insects, and wild animals ravaging the land in search of something to eat. There were earthquakes, tornadoes, blizzards, and hurricanes. The icebergs melted, causing entire landmasses to disappear."

Archangel Sandalphon mentally communicated to Archangel Michael that he must depart to bring word to the farthest reaches that all was fine. He was back in an instant, having completed his task. He spoke one word to Michael—Orion.

 Sandalphon moved toward Angie to give her something he knew she loved—an archangel hug. He knew his embrace would have a calming effect, and while he held her firmly in his enormous wingspan, he felt her relax.

Sandalphon explained, "Archangel Orion is the Archangel of the Cosmos. His portal is the center of the three stars, which make up Orion's belt. He can broadcast healing light and frequency clear out to the farthest reaches of the Universe through the center of the three stars. Angie, your proclamation sent a shockwave to the farthest reaches of the cosmos, requiring Orion to transmit a message of love and peace to all."

Next, Andrew enfolded Angie in a loving, consoling embrace. Mary and Matthew had surrounded her with their love too.

Angie bowed her head, devastated by her outburst. *They will undoubtedly send me back to the resting area after losing my temper.* 'I am so sorry. Can I take it all back? Can we rewind and start over? Please don't send me to the resting area. Please don't take me away from my friends. I can't bear it."

Remorse had dimmed Angie's light, her aura. It was Michael's turn to offer his archangel hug, which she accepted without hesitation. One by one, the Archangels, Ariel, Azrael, Chamuel, Gabriel, Haniel, Jeremiel, Jophiel, Metatron, Raguel, Raphael, Raziel, Uriel, and Zadkiel, followed Michael's example. Angie's light brightened with each embrace.

Angie loved these Archangels who radiated pure love. They sincerely wanted Angie's soul shining brightly again.

They departed in a flash, leaving Angie, Andrew, Mary, and Matthew with Michael, alone on the observation deck on the astral plane, their perch to all worlds. Everyone was eerily quiet, waiting to see what Archangel Michael would do next. *What will happen to Angie? How can we go on without her?*

Michael was first to break the silence that had descended upon them like a suffocating blanket. "Remember when you had your life reviews. Archangel Zadkiel told you that the most important thing is to forgive yourself. I am not here to judge you. You are the only one who can do that."

Angie's thoughts drifted back to when Archangel Zadkiel had wrapped his massive, strong wings around her to console her before a detailed life review. She was not perfect, and she was so sure she had messed up time after time. She had dreaded reliving any instances where she might have hurt someone else.

Angie recalled his words, "Angie, no one is here to judge you. You judge your own actions. I'm here to help you understand and to remind you not to be too hard on yourself. You will need to forgive yourself, and I'll help you do that."

Through their collective consciousness, her friends observed Angie's memory and agreed with Zadkiel's instructions. However, they knew there was no way Angie could let this go any time soon.

Chapter 2 – Thirty Days of Hell

Archangel Michael knew that Angie always wanted to find a way to forgive all souls, to give them another chance. She desperately wanted to save the non-loving souls before the shift. Forgiving herself was another matter that required swift action.

He raised his mighty sword of power and light high above his head before he slammed it down in front of him. Audible gasps choked the air. Angie and her group had never seen his display of force before.

In a calm, authoritative manner, Archangel Michael said, "I have decided that you must witness the final days on Earth. While the four of you were busy saving the loving souls and getting established on the new planet, you had no idea what was happening on the dying one. I have asked Archangel Zadkiel to be your tour guide allowing you to observe the devastation that the non-loving souls endured during those 30 days, which felt like a lifetime in their minds."

A dark, indigo-blue, glittering mist floated toward them encased in a purple glow as if on cue. "Zadkiel!" Angie yelled.

"I understand I am to take you to the School of Knowledge to see the last 30 days on Earth. It will not be a pretty sight. Let us go without delay. Please join hands." With a nod to Archangel Michael, they were off.

They found themselves in the beautiful building that housed the School of Knowledge. Their surroundings were grand. No matter how many times they had been here before, they couldn't help but stare upward toward the majestic white columns that seemed to reach beyond the heavens.

The entire area, inside and out, was bathed in a brilliant white peaceful light. Soothing instrumental music played in the background. People were milling about in total silence. Some dressed in earthly garments while others were dazzling orbs of light. Souls were free to choose their appearance. The foursome preferred clothes to be ready for their trips to visit their family on the new planet earth.

Zadkiel escorted them down a hallway lined with doors. They entered one to find the room empty—no people nor furniture. "Let's sit," said Zadkiel. Instantly chairs appeared in front of a large TV screen. Zadkiel sat in the middle chair, holding the remote control. Angie and Mary sat on either side of him with their soulmates at their sides.

A scene came into view. Angie exclaimed, "I remember this date perfectly. It was the date of the final shift of the loving souls." They could see Archangel Chamuel swirling in his leafy greenery. The stars on the outer wall gradually disappeared until there were hardly any visible. Chamuel announced that they were looking at the old planet Earth. Then, a sparkling mosaic of the brightest lights appeared before them as Chamuel announced, 'It is done.' You are observing the new planet Earth. The shift is complete."

Zadkiel reminded them, "You went to the new planet Earth and never looked back. You didn't have to. But now, you must. Thirty days of hell on Earth were let loose upon the negative souls that were left behind. Watch and observe some of what they endured."

The group was silent but wide-eyed. A birdseye overview of the planet showed total devastation. Fissures, like hungry jaws, opened upon the Earth's crust devouring everything. Vehicles and houses disappeared. Roadways abruptly ended at the edge of an abyss. Pillars of tornadoes raced around like giants bumping into each other, tearing up all that remained in their paths. Raging rivers mightily overflowed their banks. Tsunamis destroyed the coastlines leaving a littered wasteland briefly hidden on the incoming tides. Massive, swirling hurricanes hid large sections of the planet from view. Continents changed shape dividing interior lands. Farmlands were barren. Locusts devoured any greenery that managed to escape the elements. Stately trees were naked and bent like twigs. Ravenous fires raged in the blustery winds with no hope of containment. They sat in silence, watching the beautiful green Earth turn into a wasteland.

Angie exclaimed, "Florida is gone! California is gone!"

Zadkiel nodded his agreement and went on to explain, "We are now over the north pole where the icebergs have melted." Dark parcels of land emerged for the first time in millions of years.

You could hear a pin drop as Zadkiel zoomed in for a closer look at New York and the suburbs. Abandoned trucks and cars littered the highways. People had shifted out of their vehicles. The ones who remained had to leave their cars due to a lack of gas or mechanical failure. An occasional moving vehicle played bob and weave like a pinball machine. Shut down nuclear power plants explained why everything was pitch black. The scene changed to the skyscrapers where people were tripping down countless stairwells and motionless escalators. Looted shops lined the streets.

They witnessed confused people frantically calling out. No one answered because no one was there. Doorman, chauffeurs, elevator operators, and all the essential workers were gone. Cell phones were useless, and social media was idle. People were dazed and confused, running in all directions with nowhere to go. Others writhed in agony.

The fashionably dressed were reduced to rags topped with dirt-stained faces. Those who had looked down on the homeless with disdain were now living on the streets.

Zadkiel paused the documentary to explain, "Most of the working-class people shifted along with the poor and homeless. Only those lacking love in their hearts and blinded by greed remained. They had made demands on others for every aspect of their existence. Now they fended for themselves but didn't have a clue how to survive. They only knew how to lie, cheat, and steal. It didn't take long before they started to turn on each other."

"All this happened in thirty days?" asked Angie.

"Oh yes, and much more," replied Zadkiel. "Once the balance was jeopardized, the ruination of Earth, which started a long time ago, was propelled into warp speed. When greed overtook the nations and the government eliminated the environmental protections, the destructive forces accelerated. Let's watch more."

Angie asked, "Are those cats roaming the streets?"

Zadkiel chuckled. "No, Angie, those are not cats. They are rats, and as we zoom in closer, you will see cockroaches lining the walls."

They could see vultures circling in search of prey. People, lacking protection, were swatting the air at unseen bugs and threatening varmints.

"Enough! Enough!" begged Angie. "I get it. It is an awful sight. Those poor people."

"Poor people? My dear sweet Angie, have you seen enough to change your mind?" interrupted Zadkiel. "I understand you have an abundance of love in your heart. Remember, these "people" lost love in their hearts. They needed to suffer the consequences of their selfish acts. They needed to understand, to be able to judge themselves when it came time for their own life's review.

"We are not finished. You must watch more," explained Zadkiel. Alligators, crocodiles, pythons, bears, panthers, mountain lions, and more were seen roaming the inland areas searching for a meal. Wolves and coyotes were on the loose, threatening the people who were cowering in their meager shelters. Acid rains burned their skin and forced the humans and animals to fight over the few areas of refuge they could find.

"Angie? Now have you seen enough? Do you understand why thirty days was sufficient hell to pay before these non-loving souls were whisked up to the resting area?"

"Yes. I had no idea. I now understand," stated Angie.

"Okay. Let's return to Archangel Michael. He wants to do some clearing with all of you. Hold hands. Let's go."

Chapter 3 – Rejuvenation

"Surprise," Zadkiel announced as he transported the group to their favorite place, the Meet-and-Greet area. These unique personal spaces are where the departed reunite with their loved ones. Angie, Andrew, Mary, and Matthew had their private sanctuary. They could invite others if they chose to. It was their serene paradise among the stars. After watching the ruination of earth and the non-loving souls' suffering, they were happy to be here.

Angie realized that Archangel Michael was waiting for them and rushed straight into his embrace. He was instantly recognizable by his royal-blue robes and golden aura, with his stance heralding power and authority. Angie remembered the first time she saw him. His mighty presence startled her. He gently told her there was nothing to be afraid of, and there wasn't. She loved working with him. He was an excellent teacher whose helpful lessons conveyed pure love.

"I didn't know! I didn't understand! I do now. I should never have questioned you. I am very sorry. I can't apologize enough for my appalling behavior. Will you ever forgive me?"

Archangel Michael gave Angie a stern glance. "Me, forgive you? Have you learned anything?"

Angie quickly corrected herself, "I know I must forgive myself. I just want to make sure I haven't lost favor with you."

Michael announced, "It is time to undergo a cleansing to remove the built-up negativity from the horrors you just witnessed. Please form a circle with outstretched hands. Drop your hands to your sides and step back three feet. To relax, I want you to inhale deeply and exhale fully. Do this three times while you clear your minds and focus on your breath.

Standing in the middle of the circle, Archangel Michael took his mighty sword, raised it above his head, and brought it to the ground on either side of Angie. He instructed her to face right and repeated the sword movement on her front and back. He proceeded with the others and then stated, "Your negative cords are cut."

Michael then asked everyone to face forward and remain where they were. Instantly Archangel Metatron appeared in the center of the circle with his Merkabah Cube rotating above his head. It spun like a gyroscope and dazzled like a kaleidoscope. He wore deep pink and bright green to match the colors that radiated from his Cube. Metatron always reminded Angie of an intellectual college geometry professor with lots of fun toys.

"Greetings. I am here to clear your chakras. During your silence, your throat chakras have been closed. The horrible sights have impacted your eye chakras. The non-loving souls have affected your heart chakras. Witnessing the tragedies has obstructed your base chakras. We will clear all of your chakras. Please focus on your breathing."

The Cube moved over Angie's head. It slowly rotated downward to her toes. Gradually it climbed back up again until it returned to a position above her head and then glided over to Andrew. Metatron repeated the process for Andrew, Mary, and Matthew. When the Cube returned to a place over Metatron's head, he announced, "The clearing is complete." Before they could thank him, he was gone, Cube and all.

Archangel Michael instructed, "It is time to fill you with the white light of purity and peace. Welcome the light as it streams down from above. Feel it cover your entire body, inside and out, from the top of your head to beneath your toes."

Michael continued, "Your auras are once again shining brightly. Enjoy this feeling, and remember, you can do all these cleansing and clearing exercises yourself at any time by recalling these steps in your mind. Archangel Metatron and I are also available to assist you.

"It is time for all of you to return to the new planet earth. Enjoy a relaxing interlude, surrounded by your loved ones."

Matthew interrupted, "Can we stop at the dining hall before we go?"

"Not this time," announced Michael. "You will have plenty of time on your next visit. When we meet again, I will give you an in-depth explanation of the future mission, including the incarnation of the first wave of souls to the primitive planet.

As they held hands, the excitement of their homecoming overwhelmed them. They found themselves in their living room. Wendy raced to welcome them. They were in the middle of a group hug when William, her husband, ran through the door. It didn't take long for news of their arrival to telepathically spread to family members and friends far and wide. The front door banged open, time and time again, as an influx of excited well-wishers rushed in. All shared loving hugs. Being home, among loving family and friends, restored them all to the everyday joys of just feeling human.

Without hesitation, a bombardment of questions erupted. "How are you? Where have you been? Did you feel the big shutter? Do you know what caused it?" It was apparent Wendy took after Angie with her myriad of questions. She continued, "Here, sit down and let's catch up."

They quickly took their seats to avoid being lovingly smothered with more hugs and kisses. You could hear an audible sigh as the foursome telepathically but privately pondered how to answer some of the questions. *Who should begin?* They did not want to put Angie on the spot. They knew that she was still very fragile and frankly exhausted after the incident. Angie sat in complete silence.

It was Mary who decided to explain what happened without blaming Angie. "We were all with Archangel Michael when the disturbance occurred. Soon, all the Archangels arrived. We learned about a new Archangel called Orion, the Archangel of the Cosmos. Orion spread the word that everything was fine. So, you have nothing to worry about."

"What exactly caused it?" asked Wendy.

"Let's not waste any time discussing something that is of no concern." Mary turned the questioning around on the others. "How are you? What have you been doing? What's new?"

Matthew interrupted. "Why don't we go down to the town square, grab a bite, and you can share all the news?"

They all agreed and headed out the door. Only Andrew realized that Angie had remained behind.

"Andrew, please go with them. I'm exhausted, and I would like to get some rest. You go ahead," implored Angie.

He kissed her on the forehead and went out the door, supportive of her request for peace and quiet and alone time.

Angie lay down, but sleep evaded her. She tossed and turned and fluffed her pillow countless times but couldn't get her mind off what had happened. Thoughts about her outburst clouded her mind as she kept reviewing and questioning herself. Restlessness was causing her more stress. She couldn't lie there one more minute.

What could she do? Where could she go? She didn't want more questioning, which would inevitably happen if she joined the others. She loved them dearly, and they deserved to know that she caused the disruption. However, the explanation would be best coming from Andrew, Mary, and Matthew. They could help others understand much better than she could. After all, if she didn't comprehend it herself, how could she explain it to others?

She didn't want to stay in the house, risking their return before she was ready to face them. She decided to take a walk. Mindlessly, she found herself at the beach. The rays of the warm sun bounced off the gentle waves, creating multiple rainbows flashing along the shoreline. She fondly recalled the first time she met Archangel Uriel. He had come toward her adorned in bright yellow. He reminded Angie of sunbeams on a clear day, so she nicknamed him her sunshine Archangel.

The rainbows reminded her of Archangel Raziel. When she first saw him, it looked like a rainbow was sliding down from the sky right before her eyes. What a sight! The colors were brilliant and vibrant, not like the faint, pale rainbows she saw on the earthly plane. She nicknamed Raziel her Rainbow Archangel.

The rainbow memory faded as she heard seagulls off in the distance. She vaguely heard some children playing. This spot was as good as any to sit, relax, reflect, and hopefully gain some peace of mind.

Chapter 4 – Memories

Angie settled into the warm, soft sand and stared out onto the unending expanse of the sparkling ocean. She felt drained. *What did I do?* Her head dropped down to her knees as she clasped her hands around the back of her neck. *I hope no one stops and bothers me. I'm not selfish. I'm just not pleasant company right now.* She needed solitude and reflection, and she hoped that was all that she needed to get back to her old self. *My old self,* she thought. *Could that ever be possible again?*

The warmth of the sun with the repetitive rhythm of the waves mesmerized her. Before she knew it and without any prompting from a hypnotist, she was in a deep trance and traveled back in time.

She returned to the moment when she saw the bright light beckoning her. Her physical body was back on earth in a car wreck where she felt no pain. She was no longer in her body. Unconditional love filled her every pore. She wanted to race toward the light but couldn't. Twinkling, bright-white Christmas lights floated toward her. As the lights came closer and into focus, she saw a beautiful Archangel in creamy-white with a sparkling halo. His wings were enormous. Lost in her trance, as she sat on the beach, she could feel his wings encircling her in a welcoming, calming embrace just as had happened a long time ago.

This time, she knew he was Archangel Azrael. She met him many times before but had not recognized him at first. He was often known as the Angel of Death but had explained that he preferred to be known as a grief counselor. That title was much more befitting to his calm, gentle nature emanating pure love. Before he allowed her to travel toward the beckoning light, Azrael helped Angie figure out appropriate signs for her loved ones that she was leaving behind. He also helped her recall all the signs she had received from her departed loved ones.

Angie drifted deeper back in time to when she was able to follow the bright light. A feeling of relief and euphoria brought a smile to her face as she sat there. She remembered seeing her departed loved ones waving her onward. Her thoughts turned toward Archangel Jeremiel, who appeared before her to help her cross over. She remembered the golden lights sparkling around his head like a halo of shooting stars. He wore dark purple with enormous wings that encircled Angie in an Archangel hug. He had introduced himself as the Archangel of Hope with a mission to help departed souls ascend to heaven.

Her memory was crystal clear as she remained in the hypnotic trance. She found herself standing in picturesque fields filled with vividly colored flowers. Their delightful fragrances wafted on the gentle breezes. Angie gently raised her nose and inhaled as if she could smell them. The sounds of birds filled the air. Unicorns were drinking from the pond. And most importantly, all her departed loved ones were waiting to greet her.

Family, friends, pets, and her kindred spirit, Andrew, were all there in what Angie would later refer to as the Meet-and-Greet area. Everyone was doing what they loved to do. Her Dad was tending to roses, while her Mom was tending to baskets teeming with her favorite flowers. Her pets played with each other, even though they did not know each other when they lived on earth. She remembered how they bounded over to her, snuggling and loving her while her pet birds landed on her head and arms.

When she saw Andrew, she melted into his embrace. He spun her round and round and round again. She didn't want to leave him or her friends and family but soon found out she must. Archangel Jeremiel appeared before her to explain that she needed to go to the Resting Area. It is a place where every soul must transition from earth to a higher vibrational level. Her time in the Resting Area would be minimal because she lived a loving life on earth. Jeremiel assured her that everyone would be waiting for her to return. They had a banquet planned in her honor. Begrudgingly, she left with Jeremiel and found herself in a hospital ward.

The thought of her peaceful time in the Resting Area sustained her trance-like state, a state between sleeping and daydreaming. She recalled hearing wind chimes as her wake-up call when she met Archangel Jophiel, affectionately known as the Archangel of Beauty and beautiful she was. She looked like a porcelain doll adorned in an exquisite, deep-pink gown that flowed like a waterfall while it appeared to dance in the wind. Her halo of hot-pink sparkles glistened like glitter dancing around her head. Her voice sounded like a harp. In an instant, Angie was refreshed, dressed in a pretty white eye-lit gown, and was ready to return to the Meet-and-Greet area. There she found Andrew, her soulmate, waiting for her, along with all her departed loved ones.

That is where she met Archangel Ariel, the Archangel of Nature and the Outdoors. She looked like a fairy princess dressed in a pale pink gown with a crown shimmering with diamonds reflecting the sunlight in all directions. Her cheerful voice welcomed Angie. They toured the gardens together. Ariel explained that her job was to make sure everyone appreciated all living things and treated them kindly. Angie was comforted that this beautiful Archangel was in charge. She was also saddened, remembering what humans, with their free will, did to the beautiful earth. With the conflicting thoughts racing through her mind, Ariel escorted Angie to the Meet-and-Greet area and later to a chalet where she spent the night with Andrew. Her delight crept across her face in a loving smile at the thought of her pleasant memories.

All in all, she met and interacted with 15 Archangels. Mary and Matthew joined Angie and Andrew in their quest to shift the loving souls to the new earth. They incarnated as twins and married their twin counterparts, an ingenious idea designed by Metatron. Thus, they became the foursome who would work and remain together throughout time. She recalled their magical wedding and reception. The girls looked like angels without wings. They loved the bubbles that were showered on them as they left the reception; there was no wasted rice or birdseed. The bubbles glistened as they reflected the colors of double rainbows. All the Archangels helped pull off a masterpiece. The smile on Angie's face grew as these wonderful memories flashed before her like a cherished photo album.

Chapter 5 – Their Favorite Place

Suddenly, Angie was startled back to reality. "There she is!" yelled Andrew.

"Let's hurry and get to the Meet-and-Greet area!" Matthew proposed.

"What's up?" Angie asked as she wiped the sleepiness out of her eyes. "I must have dozed off. I had such a beautiful dream about the Archangels and our wedding. I hope I can return to my dream later and pick up exactly where I left off."

Andrew extended his hand to help her up and wrapped his arms around her, and whispered, "Sweetheart, Archangel Michael has summoned us to the Meet-and-Greet area. We are to spend the night there and meet him tomorrow. Remember?"

"Oh! Yes!" exclaimed Angie enthusiastically, followed by a stretch. "I've rested, and I'd love to get back up there. It fits in perfectly with the dream I just had. You were there, Andrew. You were all there."

With his arm around her waist, he nudged the group along. "Well, then. Let's get freshened up and be on our way."

They skipped down the beach and back to their family home. It was soon time to say goodbye. Promises of return visits helped overshadow the disappointing news of their departure.

"Before you go, I have something for each of you to keep as your remembrance charm." Wendy opened a gift box and revealed four pins that resembled the popular survivor ribbons surrounded by angel wings.

Wendy continued her presentation with William by her side and an audience of cheering family members. "The archangel wings symbolize your cherished archangel hugs. This white ribbon is for you, Angie. It matches the garter you wore at your wedding and is a symbol of the purity in your heart."

Angie choked back tears. She thought, *Wendy has no idea how appropriate this gift is, especially after my outburst.* "Thank you. Thank you so very much. I will wear it whenever I can."

Wendy picked up the pink ribbon. "Mary, this one is for you and represents the color of your garter. The color pink symbolizes compassion, nurturing, love, and kindness, all the traits that remind us of you. Wear it to remember us."

Mary accepted the pin and marveled at the kind words. "Oh, Wendy. How can I ever thank you? I will wear it over my heart and reach out to touch it whenever I start losing compassion and love. Thank you so much."

"And now for Andrew." Wendy went on. "Your ribbon is blue to match your wedding boutonniere. Blue symbolizes depth, stability, trust, loyalty, wisdom, confidence, intelligence, faith, and truth. You possess all these qualities and more. You are the gatherer of knowledge and wisdom. You have always been a trusted, loyal family member to Angie and us all."

Andrew wrapped his strong arms around Wendy in a sincere, loving embrace. He shook William's hand and waved to the rest of the gathering. "Thank you all. I will cherish this pin and will keep it as not only a remembrance of you, my family, and friends but to remind me to continue on my quest for knowledge. Thank you."

Andrew stepped back as Matthew moved forward. Wendy picked up the last pin in the jewelry box and said, "Last but not least, this green ribbon is for you, Matthew, to match your boutonniere. We tease you about your love of food, but there is so much more depth to you. Green symbolizes balance, life, renewal, nature, energy, harmony, freshness, safety, fertility, and the environment. You are an energetic life force in our family. We love you dearly. Wear this ribbon and be reminded of all of us."

Before the last words were out of Wendy's mouth, Matthew had surrounded her and William with a loving embrace. He extended his arms wide, encouraging the others to join in a group hug. There were tears and giggles, followed by a deep sigh.

"We had better be going," Angie, Mary, Andrew, and Matthew chimed in together.

There was a time when they would have gone to sleep and visited the astral plane during their dream times. Now that they were on the new planet earth and had a higher vibrational level, all they had to do was think about the location and transport there. When they were ready, they linked arms and put their destination into their collective minds. In an instant, they were standing with the unicorns in their private Meet-and-Greet area.

Sandalphon was there waiting for them. "Hope you weren't waiting long," Angie sang out as she ran into his embrace. "I fell asleep on the beach."

Sandalphon gave them all archangel hugs with his massive wings.

"I'm glad you had a chance to rest," replied Sandalphon. "How about some background music?"

"Absolutely," Angie replied. She had been reminiscing about their wedding. Sandalphon had put together an arrangement of perfect songs. "Good Vibrations" by the Beach Boys had played as they left the church. "Top of the World" by the Carpenters was playing as they entered the reception area. "Something" by George Harrison played for their first dance.

Angie continued. "Please play the songs you played at our wedding and more. You come up with the perfect playlists."

The others agreed. The music started playing as Angie recalled the first time she had met Sandalphon.

His aura was an enticing shade of turquoise, sparkling like a tropical ocean. Musical notes bounced around him like colorful fish frolicking on the gentle waves. A faint sound of music was in the air. He had introduced himself as the Archangel of Music and had explained that music was a prayer to heaven. He loved his task to help musicians with the tunes, with Archangel Gabriel, the Archangel of Communication, helping with the lyrics.

Angie had gone on a field trip with Sandalphon and Ariel to meet the once unseen earthly dwellers. When they visited the leprechauns, Sandalphon had serenaded them with a lilting Irish jig. Sweet flute melodies filled the air when they met the fairies. Pixies, gnomes, elves, the trees, and many more all had their perfect musical accompaniment.

On the new earth, everyone lived out in the open. Angie's mind wandered to the Wizard of Oz when the trees threw apples at Dorothy and her pals. But on the new earth, the trees gently waved their branches and spoke in soft, wise tones. Angie loved all these unique occupants of the new earth.

Memories vanished into pixie dust when Sandalphon announced he had to leave to attend to his other duties. They watched his turquoise aura disappear with musical notes trailing behind.

"What should we do first?" asked Angie, relishing in the thought that they had the rest of the day and evening to relax and enjoy their favorite place.

Mary wanted to spend some time with the unicorns. Matthew wanted to enjoy some delicious delicacies, and Andrew wanted to be with Angie. Maybe they would have a romp in the fields with their Dalmatians. They had not invited their departed friends and family to join them this day. Today was for relaxation because tomorrow, they would get back to business. Tonight, Andrew looked forward to sitting on the porch of the chalet with Angie by his side. They would gaze at the moonbeams reflecting off the lake as the twinkling stars winked at them from above.

Angie snuggled up to Andrew and whispered, "I love to come here. I remember when Ariel told me that we needed to revive our souls with nature. The outdoors calms me every time."

"Me too," agreed Mary, overhearing Angie's comment. "The colors are vibrant. I love to smell the flowers. It is so amazing to be able to smell them individually while all at the same time."

Andrew was gazing toward the babbling brook as he lazily commented, "I think my favorites are the unicorns. Look at them enjoying themselves. All animals live here in harmony, without fear. I'm glad it is like this on the new earth. Remember the first time we saw a huge lion walk past us and rub against our legs just like a house cat."

Matthew shook his head in agreement as he asked, "Can't we please stop calling it the new earth? Every time I hear that I think of the ruination of the old planet. I never want to think about that again. Let's just say 'Earth' from now on. After all, it is the only earth now that the shift has taken place."

"Agreed!" echoed Mary and Andrew.

"That settles it," exclaimed Matthew. "Let's go eat!"

"I'll be right there," Mary announced. "I want to pet the unicorns first."

"Me too," agreed Angie. "You guys go ahead. We won't be too long."

Andrew knew that the sooner they got going, the faster they would be at their private chalets. Andrew couldn't wait to relax, holding Angie in his arms.

Angie and Mary nuzzled with the unicorns and then skipped through the fields of flowers to join the others. They slipped into their dining room seats next to their mates. Plates of their favorite selections appeared before them. Soon they had their fill, and it was time to retire to their chalets. They held their partner's hand and whisked off to their porches.

Angie and Andrew rocked on the porch swings while they watched the sunset. The fireplace was ablaze and beckoned to them to come in. They plopped down on comfy pillows in each other's arms. Andrew got his wish to hold Angie tight, and Angie melted within his embrace. She was motionless, on the verge of falling asleep.

Meanwhile, Mary and Matthew were also enjoying their evening together. Soon it would be morning, and they would be meeting with Archangel Michael. Telepathically, from chalet to chalet, they wished each other goodnight.

Chapter 6 – From Paradise to the Library

Angie spent a delightful evening snuggled in Andrew's arms. Comfy pillows swallowed up the tenseness that invaded their bodies while the mesmerizing crackling fire cleared their minds.

Archangel Michael had been correct when he suggested relaxation was what they needed. Sunbeams, peaking through the windows, was nature's alarm clock letting them know it was time to start this new day. Angie and Andrew knew where they would find Mary and Matthew. They freshened up, joined hands, and whisked over to the dining hall. Matthew already had a plate of his favorite goodies piled high before him. Mary was sampling a few choice morsels.

Mary looked up and extended a greeting. "Good morning. Did you have an enjoyable evening?"

"Yes, we did," responded Angie. "It was very restful, and I'm anxious to find out about the details of our next mission." Andrew was nodding in agreement.

"Not so fast, Angie," Matthew interjected. "Let's finish our meal first and then set a spell by the lake while our food digests."

"Of course," agreed Angie. As she thought of pancakes smothered with fresh strawberries, a plate appeared before her. "Yum." She glanced over toward Andrew to find his plate overflowing with his favorites. He had already dug in. The smirk on his face revealed that he was thoroughly enjoying himself.

Soon they had their fill and ran out the door and down the hill toward the lake, giggling the entire way. The wind tussled their hair and pushed at their backs. They were like little children even though they had amassed a wealth of wisdom through many lifetimes. Childlike fun was therapeutic at any age. It was a beautiful day like every day in the Meet-and-Greet area; it was picture-perfect.

Angie reminisced aloud. "There is nothing like spending time with nature. The colorful sights, enjoyable sounds, and aromatic fragrances are delightful. I know we have all of this on the new earth, but there is nothing like coming back to the place where we witnessed Paradise for the first time."

The others nodded in agreement as Matthew piped in. "And the food!"

The others laughed. They didn't need to eat to nourish their bodies, but they all loved to partake in the deliciousness. Matthew added, "The best part is you can eat as much as you want and never gain any weight."

Amid the giggles, Mary suggested, "Let's go say goodbye to the unicorns before we get back to work." As she flung her arms around their necks, they returned her affection while being careful not to hurt her with their stately horns. Angie caught up next with Andrew and Matthew, fast on her heels.

Andrew reached over and squeezed Angie's hand. In the silence of their thoughts, they could read each other's minds as they dreamily remembered another time when they shared experiences in this incredible place. Their emotions had soared as they pledged their eternal love for one another. At this moment, they were renewing that pledge once again, sealed with a kiss.

These majestic animals enjoyed all the attention. Unicorns had vanished from the old earth. Although they were prevalent on the New Earth, these two were special. They were the original ones the foursome had observed, and these would forever hold a special place in their hearts.

Angie, Andrew, Mary, and Matthew plopped down on the grass to enjoy the scenery for a little longer. The babbling brook, the unicorns, the birds' songs, and the scents of the flowers wafting in on the breezes were enchanting.

Telepathically, they received their next instructions from Archangel Michael. He wanted to meet them outside the Library on the astral plane. Angie loved books and had always wanted to read every single one in the entire world. She had thought that was impossible until she visited this unique Library. There, all writings became part of your memory. You could easily and quickly gather the knowledge of every single book ever written.

They linked their arms, thought about the Library, and instantly transported there.

Archangel Michael was waiting outside the door and carefully studied them, especially Angie. He noticed that their vibrations were shining brightly, even more brightly than before. He spoke. "I can see that your visit back home and to the Meet-and-Greet area has done wonders. So, let's get started. Before we go in, I would like to recap the situation. Let's sit comfortably on these benches."

In his patient, scholarly fashion, Archangel Michael started his story with the mission to save the loving souls. "As you are aware, most of the population on earth was loving and made the shift to the new planet earth. All four of you played a crucial role in that transition, and the archangels acknowledge your great accomplishment. The loving souls are deservedly enjoying life with enhanced benefits."

The group nodded their heads in agreement as Michael continued. "There was a much smaller percentage that had lost their way. Instead of letting genuine love guide them, they turned to greed and power. They persuaded others to follow them. Those followers lost love in their hearts and believed that they would be better off following a loveless path. They had listened to the negative voice of their egos."

When the group agreed, Michael said, "Some souls were more severely damaged than others. The worst of the worst are still in the resting area and will be there for a very long time. They were the corrupt, greedy leaders. Dictators worldwide continue to rest, which is necessary to restore love to their negative souls. They need to prepare for the intense counseling that will follow. Many will argue, blame others, and continue to believe that they lived a good life. Some will not advance despite counseling. They will have to return to the resting area until they have achieved the position where they will be ready for counseling. They must realize that they were wrong, very, very wrong. Most importantly, they must acknowledge that their actions hurt others.

"Many followers have damaged their karma to a lesser degree. They were victims. The pull toward negativity had been too strong to resist. They convinced themselves that they were on the right path as they were spiraling downward. Their life purpose must be love. Love of self. Love of fellow man. Love of all creatures, from the largest to the most minute. Love of the environment."

Lost in their thoughts of love, Michael changed the mood with this question, "Who is up for a field trip? All souls must visit the Library, the Tapestry Room, and the School of Wisdom. Let's go visit these areas to remind us of the journey these souls must go through before they are allowed to incarnate to the primitive planet." Michael opened the door to the Library allowing the others to enter before him.

Chapter 7 – Library and Tapestry Rooms

Archangel Michael led the way through the reception area. When he approached the Library entrance, he offered greetings to an archangel who was waiting for them.

"Archangel Jeremiel," Angie called out as she ran into his arms. He wrapped his mighty wings around her. "You are the Angel of Hope. You helped me, and I am forever grateful."

Golden starlight radiated around his dark-purple robe. His primary task is to help souls see their life's loving purpose. He had brought Angie through the light and escorted her to a reception with her departed loved ones. Later, he had brought her to the resting area.

While Jeremiel turned to embrace the others, Angie glanced around the Library. She loved this place. Some people walked around carrying books, manuscripts, and scrolls, which wasn't necessary since knowledge imprints on your mind. Once she learned about imprinting, Angie's thirst for reading brought her here often. Her vast knowledge base did not slow down her endless questions. She wanted to know everything.

Michael and Jeremiel led the way down a hallway where emeralds, rubies, crystals, and other precious stones adorned the walls. They reflected light from the windows above like a dazzling kaleidoscope gently spinning around the room.

The group entered the main Library with a cathedral ceiling, multiple seating areas, and rooms along the perimeter. There were precious gems on the interior walls that gave off plenty of light. Gentle background music softened the atmosphere. There were no computers, laptops, iPads, printers, or electronic devices anywhere, and no one was taking notes.

They nodded to the Guardian of the Library of Knowledge, who wore a robe and held a beautiful, functional pointer. He led them to a massive book on a pedestal table.

"The *Akashic Record Book*!" Angie exclaimed. "It contains the records of everyone's past lives. I need to see how my record looks after my unfortunate outburst."

Jeremiel explained, "as you know, the *Akashic Record Book* is ever-changing. First, let's look at Angie's Akashic Record." The Guardian of the Library, who accompanied them, directed his pointer toward the book. The pages flipped with a wild abandon and then abruptly stopped at precisely the correct page, Angie's page.

Angie hesitantly looked and was happily surprised. There was a large entry about saving the loving souls and a trivial notation when she lost her temper. The record concluded that she had repented for the outburst.

"Wow. I was concerned I had tainted my record forever," commented Angie.

Jeremiel responded by saying, "Angie, remember that this book records incidents and does not pass judgment. As the Archangel of Hope, I will remind you that there is hope for all souls. Your incident might have sent reverberations throughout the Universe, but you did not hurt anyone. You reacted out of love and compassion for the souls that suffered damage. You must forgive yourself. That said, it doesn't permit you to repeat that incident."

Archangel Michael spoke up. "The archangels have been working with the damaged souls. The candidates for the first wave of the incarnation have witnessed and acknowledged the error of their ways. Please point out some of their records."

The Guardian directed his pointer toward the book. Pages cascaded in waves and abruptly stopped short, illustrating both adverse and newly recorded positive incidents. *It is reassuring that there is hope for their futures,* thought Angie.

"Jeremiel, please show them the entries of some of the severely damaged souls," instructed Michael. Again, the rustling pages flipped quickly but with purpose, landing on individual pages. Substantial entries indicated the wrongdoings, emphasizing the lack of love and the hurt done to others. The description ended with a statement that the soul had not yet atoned for these actions. Angie recognized the name of one of the worst offenders and was relieved that he was still in the resting area. He had only loved himself and caused worldwide strife contributing to the ruination of the planet.

"May I ask a question?" Angie piped up. Archangel Michael nodded. "You say there is hope for all souls. What about the very damaged souls. Will they ever be allowed to live among the loving souls."

Archangel Michael explained, "Every soul must have the chance to find the loving path. Even the most severely damaged ones. Your challenge will be to help all of them with the assistance of the archangels."

"I don't know if I can do that. I don't know if I am strong enough to conquer that much evil and hatred," advised Angie.

"Yes, you are, Angie. You are stronger than you think. The negativity will be gone by the time you are invited to help. However, once they go through the Veil of Forgetfulness, they may need nudging to keep them on the loving path. You are capable of doing that."

Angie felt encouraged.

Michael announced, "I'll give you a moment to research your records, Andrew, Mary, and Matthew, and then we will move to the Tapestry Room."

While she waited, Angie thought about the Tapestry Room. When she first heard of the room, Angie had expected to find material bolts with sewing machines buzzing. She later realized that it had been a silly notion since clothing was optional on the astral plane. Clothing is selected by thought. One could also elect to appear as energy.

Angie was snapped back to reality when Archangel Jeremiel bid them farewell.

Archangel Michael led the way to the Tapestry Room, where another archangel waited for them. "I'll leave you for now but will meet you later at the School of Wisdom."

"Raziel," Angie exclaimed, "My Rainbow Archangel! You always arrive with a beautiful, brightly colored rainbow appearing to fall from the sky. You told us you created rainbows as a pause break so busy people would run outside and look up, if only for a few minutes during their busy days.

"Greetings, my friend, and greetings to all of you. I am privileged to escort you to the Tapestry Room. Come with me," Raziel said.

They gazed at the enormous tapestry, which was about twenty-five feet tall and a mile or so wide. It circled the room and seemed to go on forever. Light from the upper windows and crystal-studded chandeliers illuminated the threads. Some of the tapestry strands were very thin, like pieces of string, while others were as thick as cables. The strands' sections were in beautiful shades of red, orange, yellow, green, blue, indigo, and violet to match Raziel's rainbows.

Raziel reminded them, "Each color represents the spiritual energy of the soul at a specific time. The black areas signify a period when a soul ventured off life's loving path. When souls come to view their strands, they can see their progress or failures illustrated by the size and brilliance of the strands' colors. When they plan for their next incarnation, they devise ways to enrich their souls.

"Notice how each thread crosses and touches other strands that intersect with even more strands. Every soul has a direct influence on all the souls it touches, causing a ripple effect. The tapestry is forever changing. All humanity is affected by the actions of one."

The Guardian of the Tapestry Room had joined them. His pointer was elegant. He pointed to Angie's cord. She was afraid to look, but she knew she had to. To her surprise, it was still brightly colored. She looked inquisitively at Raziel.

Raziel responded to her silent surprise. "Angie, the cords show the impact you have on others. You did not hurt anyone or foster any negativity toward humanity with your outburst. Your love for all those who were adversely affected by the negative souls runs deep."

"Whew. I'm so glad my cord was not affected. I promise I will never lose my temper again," confirmed Angie. "Seeing this means so much to me."

"It is my pleasure to help such a loving soul and one that loves my rainbows," Raziel replied.

Raziel said, "The primary purpose of our visit here is not to see your cords but to see the cords of the first wave of souls that will incarnate to the farthest reaches of the galaxy. The Guardian pointed to several cords that had been extraordinarily dark but were gradually starting to turn lighter. These were the candidates for the first wave of the incarnation. They have seen and acknowledged the error of their ways. Because we can all read each other's minds telepathically, they cannot hide their true feelings.

"Now, we must meet Archangel Michael in the School of Wisdom." They joined hands and were off.

Chapter 8 – School of Wisdom

In a flash, they were standing on the steps of the School of Wisdom. Raziel bid them farewell, and they watched his colorful rainbow vanish from sight.

Archangel Michael was waiting for them with another archangel. Michael explained, "I have asked Uriel to join us. He will help you focus your mind on receiving all the knowledge, wisdom, and understanding that will be beneficial for the next mission."

"My Sunshine Angel," Angie proclaimed, stepping forward, smiling, and greeting him. She didn't wait for an invitation as she rushed into his archangel hug. He was adorned in bright yellow, including his aura, and always reminded Angie of sunbeams on a clear day. He circled the group with hugs for all.

"I've been asked here to protect you and illuminate your mind with information, ideas, epiphanies, and insights. Although I love to be called Angie's Sunshine Archangel, I am also considered a wise old owl." At this, Angie smiled.

"Come with me." Archangel Michael led Uriel and the others to the area where they could hold a private meeting.

The area was magnificent. The walls were full of precious stones of every color. There were private rooms and open spaces where people were communicating in hushed tones or telepathically. The ceiling was very tall, with a rotunda high above seeming to reach the heavens. Light from the windows illuminated the area below. Sunlight bounced off the gemstones that radiated all the colors of the rainbow.

Michael began. "The repentant souls, the candidates, have spent exhaustive hours in the School of Wisdom, doing research to help them understand how to make wise future choices. They carefully mapped out their life plans. They sat before the council to have their proposal reviewed, altered and approved. In their desire to quickly repair their karma, some have devised very aggressive strategies. These plans could lead to failure, in their minds, if they are not 100% successful. Some ideas are modified to be more realistic."

Michael continued. "Loving souls are living on the new earth. If their soulmate turned dark, they were not allowed to incarnate together and are separated. New bonds will form when they match with others

"The first wave will be transported to the primitive planet as families and will not go through the birthing process. They have met with the archangels and determined their role in the family unit. Some will be mothers, fathers, and children encompassing a variety of ages. Families will marry outside their lineage. A detailed timeline has been devised for future souls to join the families by birth.

"On this planet, they will go through the Veil of Forgetfulness. As you know, that means that regardless of the plans they have made on the astral plane, they will not have any recollection. They will also have free will and egos. All these are needed as teaching tools. These are the same conditions on the old planet earth. We hope that they will always choose the loving path. The archangels are helping with the final details, and part of the plan includes your guidance."

Michael found his audience intently listening, so he continued. "Now, I will explain where we are sending them. We have an uninhabited planet in the very distant realm of the universe. It is similar to the old planet earth before it received its very first occupants. There is breathable air, freshwater, vegetation, animals, oceans, along with caves to be used for dwellings. It will be a primitive existence deplete of all conveniences. Consider it a teaching school of the most basic type. Originally it was going to be referred to as the Planet of Souls or PoS for short. However, I have learned that the acronym 'pos' has a different connotation."

A smile spread over the faces of those in attendance as the meaning, 'piece of sh—' came to mind. "Yes, the name may be perfect for these negative souls after what they did to their planet. I did see you grin. However, there is no reason for these people to smile. The planet will be called Tenalp, the lost planet in the farthest reaches of the universe. The inhabitants will be the souls that lost their way."

Matthew, who typically only spoke when he was hungry, interrupted. "Can't we find a better name for the new earth? Every time I hear that I think of the ruination of the old earth. I don't want to ever think about that again. I want to think of Paradise. We have discussed it and would like to call the new planet 'Earth' from now on. After all, it is the only earth now that the shift has taken place."

Michael could see Angie, Andrew, and Mary vigorously nodding their heads in agreement as he contemplated the idea and commented. "I believe we need an entirely new name. Earth is earth, and the name conjures up memories of both the old and new earth. The words' old' and 'new' distinguish them. I will take this valuable suggestion under advisement and consult with the other archangels." The discussion of the name change ended with nods of understanding from the foursome.

Chapter 9 – A Word to the Wise

"What is next?" Angie asked.

She was not expecting a reply but was thrilled when Michael answered. "Remember when you wanted to take a vacation after the shift? We agreed, and we asked all of you to help us identify any negative souls that may have infiltrated the New Earth. Although we had not suspected any, we needed confirmation, and you confirmed all was well."

Michael could see his audience reflecting as he continued. "No one goes through the Veil of Forgetfulness, so all souls remember and can achieve their life's purpose. Free will is limited to kind-hearted choices. Telepathic, compassionate communication has replaced Egos. All these changes, made in honor of the loving souls, have yielded a planet full of love, kindness, and cooperation."

Angie responded on behalf of the group. "We enjoyed our vacation. It was wonderful to live among a planet full of loving souls and confirm that the shift was a total success."

"Thank you, Angie." Archangel Michael said. "You have all had the experience of recognizing and confirming that souls continue on their loving path. The occupants of Tenalp will go through the Veil of Forgetfulness, have loving and non-loving free-will choices, and they will have egos without telepathic communication. They must start at the beginning of time.

"Therefore, Tenalp is going to need monitoring and observation. You will have access to the Akashic records and the Tapestry of Life. However, personal visits to the planet will also prove very helpful. It has been a very long time since any of you dwelled on a primitive planet and have had to fend for yourselves."

Angie could not contain herself. "Are we going to live on the primitive planet?"

Michael explained, "No. You will dwell on the spacecraft with Legna. You will be in human form and be able to visit the planet as observers."

"Whew!" Angie momentarily forgot that everyone could hear her as they read her mind.

"I must know that I can count on all of you in our plans to start sending the most deserving souls to Tenalp. May I hear your affirmative responses?"

One after another, they gave their commitment, assuring Michael they could be counted on and would do their best. As Michael scanned their thoughts, he only noticed one question, and that was 'when.' *When was this to take place?*

Legna. Angie's thoughts drifted back to the first time she saw this magnificent ET. *He resembled an archangel without wings, halo, or an aura. He was tall and stately and exuded power. His protective covering was pure white with large oval eyes. They didn't need ears because they read minds. They had been everywhere, walking the earth and filling the sky but went undetected with very few exceptions. They were able to bend time, returning people to the same time that they had left earth. Cloaking devices hid their ships. On the New Earth, the various communities of ET's lived among the humans in perfect harmony. Their large spacecraft were parked in the airports and hovered above for all to see. She remembered Michael telling her not to be afraid of them or how they looked. They came in all shapes and sizes and possessed different skill levels. He explained that they were devoted to helping. Angie sensed pure lovingness whenever she was with them.*

Michael knew they were thinking about the ET's. It was time to focus on the task at hand. "In answer to your collective question, 'when,' we will let you know. First, you will return to New Earth for a vacation to enjoy visits with your family and friends. Once the mission on Tenalp starts, it will be intense, and free time will be scarce. When I am ready for you, I'll let you know. There are more archangels I want you to meet who have different tasks to help you with this future mission."

"More archangels? Wow. I didn't know there were any more," stated Angie.

Michael responded. "There are multitudes of archangels who you will meet and interact with over time. You have worked with 15 of us who primarily watch over Earth. You will meet more who keep an eye on the universe and will help develop Tenalp. They are aware of your successes.

"Now off with you. Your family will be thrilled. Enjoy, and wait to hear from me."

Archangel Uriel bid them farewell, and they watched as this glittering sunlight angel vanished from view.

Archangel Michael gave them all individual archangel hugs, and he was gone

Without further delay or discussion, the foursome held hands and collectively thought of home and instantly found themselves back on the new planet earth.

Chapter 10 – Home Sweet Home

"We're home!" announced Angie, Andrew, Mary, and Matthew. They were standing in the living room of their first home, which had stayed in the family for generations.

Andrew, in his take-charge manner, hollered, "Hello? Hello? Is anyone home?"

Everyone quieted. With heads tilted upward as if their ears could pick up sounds better, they listened intently to... silence.

"Nobody's home," Mary said dreamily, "Remember when we first saw this house and fell in love with it?"

Angie reminisced, "Oh, yes. Remember the library room full of books from floor to ceiling?"

Mary replied, "Yes, I remember. I had to pull you away to see the kitchen. When we saw the large dining table, we started planning family dinners."

Andrew interrupted, "Matthew and I had to drag you away from the kitchen to show you the upstairs bedrooms with their separate sitting rooms.

Mary laughed, "Figures you guys would find the bedrooms. I must admit they were perfect for us."

Matthew, who had remained silent, added his thoughts, "Separate bedrooms with their sitting rooms made it feel like two apartments. It was nice having you guys close, but there were times when—"

"Christmas!" Angie said. "Remember deciding where to put the Christmas tree so the lights would shine onto the porch creating a fantasyland?"

"I sure do!" said Mary. "Remember imagining a wreath for the front door and garland for the staircase? This house became our "home" the first time we saw it."

"And it always will be!" agreed Angie.

They wandered out onto the porch and were rocking on the swings, reminiscing, and enjoying the quiet.

Angie got up and walked to the head of the stairs and asked, "What do you guys think about the next mission? How can we help keep souls on the loving path?"

Andrew got up and put his arm around Angie. Mary grabbed her hand and said, "we are in this together, so don't worry. The archangels will guide and help us. Let's have some fun! We are on vacation. Let's put this out of our mind for now."

Andrew pulled Angie and Mary close, and Matthew came over to join in a group hug. Their loving moment was quickly interrupted.

"Hey, guys. How are you? When did you get here? I'm so glad you are back home!" Wendy shattered the silence with a barrage of questions as she ran up the front walkway. "Come to the kitchen. I'll get us some coffee, tea, anything? Whatever you want."

"How about some cider? suggested Matthew. "Let's celebrate Fall. It might not get cold in this southern climate, but we can still enjoy the tastes of the seasons."

"Agreed," confirmed Wendy. "I suppose I won't have to beg you to taste some freshly baked apple cider doughnuts while we catch up."

They headed toward the kitchen and found their favorite chairs. A plate of doughnuts circled the table while Wendy poured the cider.

A chorus of "hellos" was heard resounding through the living room.

"In here!" yelled Wendy. "Come see our guests and join us."

"Wow!" exclaimed William. Everyone hugged and kissed. "The kids, grandkids, and I were checking out a new spacecraft that landed this morning."

Enthusiastic comments rang out: "You should have seen it!" "It is awesome!" It is more majestic than any other saucer-like spacecraft we have ever seen!"

Angie thought back. *We often observed, spent time on, and traveled on the advanced crafts formerly known as UFOs. They are engineering marvels.*

Wendy interrupted Angie's thoughts, "There is plenty of time to check out the new crafts. Let's find out how long our guests can stay, what news they have from the astral plane, and the far-off universes."

Everyone quieted down for a brief moment while they waited in anticipation of tales from beyond. The answers did not come fast enough, and another barrage of questions from competing voices rose above the din. "What have you guys been up to?" "How long can you stay?" "Will you have time to see the new ship with us?"

Angie's voice rose above the crescendo, "We have a fascinating mission ahead of us which will take us to a primitive planet in the farthest reaches of the Universe. The mission could take a very long time, and probably right through the holidays."

This time, Wendy added her disappointed voice to the mix, "Oh No! You have always made it back home for the holidays. It won't be the same without you."

Voices chimed in, "What is the name of the planet?" "Who lives there?" "Can we come to visit you there?" "Can't you pop in for the actual holiday?" "What is the planet like?"

"Okay. Okay. One at a time, please. We know! We will miss all of you too!" Mary gently replied. "We can have a special celebration when we return. You will always be in our hearts, thoughts, and prayers."

Wendy sadly added," Same here, but we'll miss hugs and kisses, and it will be so lonely without you. But let's not get upset and spoil this visit. Who knows what could happen by the time the holidays roll around? Let's talk about now. Please, tell us about the mission."

Andrew continued with the explanation. "A new virgin planet exists in the farthest reaches of the Universe. It is time for some souls to start living there, and we will assist with the colonization."

"That sounds so exciting!" interjected William. "Please tell us more. Will the archangels be helping too?"

Angie confirmed, "Yes, the archangels will be helping us. We will meet some new archangels too."

"New ones!" "Who are they?" "Will we get to meet them too?" Angie had paused to let the comments die down and then said, "We haven't met them yet. We did hear about one named Orion, who is the Archangel of the Cosmos. I'm sure, in time, you will get to meet them."

With a note of sorrow in her voice, Wendy asked, "How long before you leave?"

Angie jumped in to squelch the sadness before it took hold. "We will be able to stay for a while. We will have time to visit the fairies, leprechauns, and the mighty trees."

The clamoring took an uptick as new questions emerged. "Will Ariel and Sandalphon be with you again?" "Will we get to see them?" "I love Sandalphon's musical notes." "And I love his music." "Ariel is so much fun too." "Have you visited the fairies in our backyard?"

"Yes! No!" Angie tried to answer their questions and decided it was better to address them one at a time. "Ariel and Sandalphon will meet us here. You will get to see them again. No, I have not seen your fairy dwellers yet."

Wendy suggested, "Let's visit together after dark when the fairies wake from their daytime sleep."

Angie had tears of joy and instantly agreed. "Yes. I would love to see them and see what you have done to liven up their home."

"Now that that's settled, tell us more about this new mission. We would all love to know more details." Wendy turned the conversation back to the group.

Andrew continued. "There is no one living on the planet right now. Some family units will transport there. They will live in caves and learn how to catch and prepare their food. You have heard about the cavemen who inhabited the old earth a very long time ago. Well, that is how this planet will begin."

"Will there be dinosaurs?" "Will there be unicorns?" "Will there be any stores or restaurants?"

Angie jumped into the barrage of questions. "No, no, no, no. No dinosaurs. No unicorns. No stores. No restaurants. If you want to understand more, read up on the cavemen of ancient history."

Before the questions could overtake the conversation once again, Andrew took a quick breath and continued. "We will not live on the planet but instead will live on an advanced spacecraft and the astral plane, and we will transport to the planet when we are needed. I'm sure we will have plenty of stories to tell the next time we come to visit."

The conversations continued as the foursome took turns explaining what little they knew about the mission and how the most deserving rehabilitated souls were ready to incarnate. Children, grandkids, and great-grandkids came and went interrupting conversations with hugs and kisses as they helped themselves to cider and doughnuts.

Angie had to admit she loved being back home with her family. *The future will be something to think about later,* she thought.

Chapter 11 – Backyard Fairyland

Tall shadows painted an ominous landscape as nightfall consumed the fading sunlight. Everyone gathered on the porch with flashlights in hand. The procession gingerly moved around to the back of the house, carefully finding their footing on the flagstones that paved the way. Wendy stepped to the side to light the Tiki torches that rimmed the yard.

Right before their eyes, the backyard turned magical, reflecting the dancing firelight of the mini torch fires. Fairies stretched in their colorful flower petal beds. As they arose, so did their shadows, giving the appearance of giants instead of the wee fairies they were. Soon the stretching illusions vanished as the fairies took flight, darting faster than their shadows could keep up.

Nightfall meant it was time for the fairies to rejoice in their nighttime merriment. They would dance and play until dawn's early light when they would contently collapse in their flower petals to sleep the day away.

Angie fondly remembered when a fairy, dressed in yellow, was caught in some Jasmin vines. Mary had helped her snip those vines to free the wee darling. That was when the fairies realized that the young girls could see them by looking through a Mason jar bottom. A lifelong friendship was formed that day.

Over time, they no longer needed the special glass to see their friends. In later years, the fairies had moved to this same house with the adult girls and their guys. They lived in the tool shed and surrounding gardens. During a hurricane, they were moved inside the house until it was safe to go outside. Potted plants and flowers dug from the gardens were brought inside to give the fairies a place to sleep. Stone circles decorated on the floor where the fairies could continue with their nighttime activities during the storm.

Angie congratulated Wendy when she returned from lighting up the yard. "The gardens are beautiful. You have planted every shape, size, and color imaginable. The backyard is a botanical work of art worthy of a flower show."

"Thank you," acknowledged Wendy. "The fairies have expressed their delight with every new planting. I love my hobby and am glad to do it. Love and care go into every selection. There are Hibiscus, Roses, and Allamanda. For the smaller fairies, there are Impatiens and Vinca in shades of pink and white. For the newborns, we have Snapdragons. The Bougainvillea bushes add a deep fuchsia color but not for sleeping because of the thorns.

"I love this garden paradise!" commented Mary. "The Snapdragon nursery is divine.

While they stood there, enraptured in the magical fantasyland, a fairy in a yellow gown flit around their shoulders. Without hesitation, the girls recognized the fairy they had rescued when they were children. "Sunny!" they cried out in unison. Soon the other childhood fairies, wiping the sleep from their eyes, joined the happy reunion.

"Hi, Sunny!" Mary called out. "It is great to see you again."

"Yes, it is," confirmed Angie. "We are anxious to see how Wendy has decorated inside the shed."

With Sunny leading the way, the fairies flew in through an open window, disappearing into the darkness within. Wendy led the larger folk through the door and asked them to wait while crystal lights slowly came to life, bathing the room in a faint glow. Silky, colorful scarves adorned the walls shimmering in the breezes wafting through the open windows. Small statues of fairies and angels decorated the shelves and surfaces. Colorful flower plaques graced the walls. There were rock circles in the corners of the floor for their dances. It was a safe and welcoming haven to keep their friends dry when the nightly rains came.

Angie recalled, *It only rains at night on the new earth, filling the reservoirs with nutrient-rich drinking water capable of sustaining life and making food optional.*

Angie endearingly showered Wendy with admiration. "This is marvelous. You thought of everything—soft lighting, gentle breezes, and pretty decorations. I love it."

"I love it too," agreed Mary. "All that is missing is a unicorn or two."

They all giggled at the thought of unicorns fitting in the small shed. Sunny and the other fairies flew out the window, signaling it was time to be outdoors frolicking with their friends.

"Let's go join them," announced Wendy. The procession practically skipped out the door.

It was customary for the fairies to dance on the ground within their stone circles but dangerous when the humans were among them. The fairies had learned, a long time ago, that they could dance with these giant beings if they danced around their shoulders. That is how they danced on this night. Wind chimes provided the music. Some fairies had flutes that the big folk could barely hear, but there was no doubt the fairies heard them. Everyone danced, switching partners and fairy groups as the night wore on.

"I'm getting hungry." Without turning to look, they all knew that Matthew had uttered that statement. "I would like to go downtown to grab a bite to eat. Anyone else?"

"Let's go and leave the fairies to enjoy their evening," directed Wendy as she led the way.

"Thank you, Wendy, for a magical night," Angie acknowledged as they linked arms and proceeded down the roadway to the town center.

"You are all welcome to come to visit the fairies at any time," assured Wendy.

As they strolled down the roadway, they passed one of the fields, teaming with flowers, butterflies, and birds, getting ready to shelter for the night. There was a group of unicorns headed inside. When Mary called 'Hello,' they turned and galloped back, all trying to nuzzle her at once. Soon the others caught up and joined in. Love was in the air as they cuddled with their old friends.

Matthew practically pleaded with Mary, "Come on. Time to go. You will have plenty of time to revisit the unicorns."

"I know what you want," stated Mary as she reluctantly turned to go. "See you soon." As if they understood and probably did, the unicorns turned and raced back to the barn.

As they neared the town square, music and laughter filled the air, drowning out the private conversations. Twinkling white lights decorated the gazebo.

"Let's sit outside on the benches," suggested Mary. "It is too beautiful to stay indoors.

Matthew immediately chimed in, "I'll play waiter and bring out the food."

While they waited, the magic continued in the company of those they loved as they sat in silence, enjoying their surroundings. They were all remembering times past.

There was a large field next to the gazebo, ringed with trees decorated with twinkling lights. The tree lighting display was switched off. Before their eyes, millions of fireflies performed a synchronized mating show. The males rapidly flashed their lights. When they stopped, the area was pitch black for a couple of seconds. Then the females lit up the night with their graceful lights, swirling this way and that until they stopped, throwing the area into darkness. The fireflies repeated this mating ritual over and over again to the delight of the mesmerized spectators.

Soon the tempting smell of pizza tickled their noses, returning them to the present time. "Here you go. Dig in." offered Matthew as he passed out plates and napkins. They all grabbed a slice or two.

Angie remarked. "I love making new memories with all of you, and this night has brought forth magical memories that I will cherish forever."

Chapter 12 – Old Friends

"Yum," Angie's sleepy utterance was followed by, "I'm starving." *Matthew must be up.* A delicious aroma found its way over from the kitchen, awakening those hoping to catch a couple of extra winks.

When they returned home from the gazebo and firefly display, they collapsed into a deep sleep. Getting washed up was a hurried event, with the delectable scents luring them toward the kitchen.

"Good morning," Wendy cheerily greeted them. "Sit. We have plenty of food and many choices. Help yourselves."

Mary asked, "Matthew, how did you get down here without us hearing you? And, Wendy, we didn't hear the children leave."

Wendy replied, "I reminded the kids not to bang the door. As for Matthew, he has a great nose for food. He was so quiet. He even startled me when he showed up at the kitchen table."

An occasional clang of silverware broke the silence. When the diners couldn't eat another morsel, they contentedly sat back, except Matthew, who made sure no food went to waste.

"Tomorrow, Sandalphon and Ariel will be joining us," announced Angie. "We should plan some fun-filled adventures for today. Maybe we can check out that new spacecraft." Their chairs scraped against the floor as they headed back to their room to get organized.

Suddenly, the curtains fluttered into a gentle frenzy. The faint sound of music filled the room, floating in on the breezes. They glanced at each other as their smiles stretched from ear to ear, and their eyes twinkled in anticipation. Andrew announced, "Sandalphon." They practically tripped over each other as they ran through the living room and out onto the porch, where Wendy also joined them.

Joyously, Angie was the first to throw herself into his waiting archangel hug. "I missed you. I'm so glad we will be spending time together." The others practically had to pull her away to get their hugs. Musical notes filled the air, bouncing around on the love shared by all.

Questions burst forth. "Weren't you supposed to come tomorrow?" "Are you early?" "Where is Ariel?" "Is she late?" "Wasn't she supposed to come with you?" "Are you going to stay with us today?" "What are the plans?"

"Where do I begin?" pondered Sandalphon. "Ariel will be here tomorrow. I arrived at exactly the right time. I plan to spend the day with you locally, and then tomorrow, we will go on an adventure."

Amid a chorus of jubilant responses, more questions erupted. "What are we going to do today? Is anyone going to join us?"

Sandalphon announced, "Today, I am your guide. I would like to see the fairy community in your backyard and the trees surrounding the firefly arena. I understand there are Weeping Willows, Quaking Aspen, and mighty oaks. But those are nighttime activities. Let's visit the new spacecraft since you will be spending a great deal of time aboard this magnificent ship.

Andrew had questions. "When our mission starts, are we going to stay on the new craft parked on the airfield? Some of our family members have been talking about it. Will we be able to go onboard today?"

"Correct on both counts. Legna was unable to be here. However, crew members are ready for us. Why don't you walk down so you can say hello to the unicorns again, and I'll meet there?" He winked at Mary and was off.

At the mention of unicorns, Mary encouraged the party to leave without delay. "We need time to visit the pasture, and we need plenty of time to investigate the new ship that will be our home away from home. Let's go now!"

Wendy decided to remain behind to get some chores done. The rest of the group practically ran down the road. The unicorns were waiting as if they knew their friends were coming. They hugged, nestled, and frolicked. Watching their antics resulted in belly laughs that had them collapsing on the ground as they tried to catch their breath. Laughter filled the air.

Andrew, the timekeeper of the group, broke the spell. "It is time to go. Sandalphon will be waiting for us, and if we want to explore every part of our future but temporary home, we must leave now."

They stood, dusting off their clothes, and enjoyed a parting hug with their majestic, horned friends.

The airport came into view. It took a moment to realize what they were seeing. There was an image of a bright blue sky with puffy white clouds sitting on the airfield as if it had fallen from the sky.

"Look! The aircraft is reflecting the sky above. I wonder how they do that. Does the reflection continually change? Yes, it does!" Angie answered her question as the clouds shifted to mirror the sky above. "Let's hurry."

They ran to the sleek shiny craft, admiring it, gazing at the captured reflections, touching it, and scurrying around it. They couldn't find any stairs or doors to enter. As they thought of transporting inside, stairs materialized before their eyes.

"Let's check this out," Matthew said. He led the way, probably wondering if there was anything to eat inside.

The stairs vanished once the last of the party stepped inside. Sandalphon greeted them in an enormous corridor that seemed to encircle the ship. "Hello, and welcome. You could have transported in, but I wanted you to experience the magnificent stairs. Come, and I'll introduce you to our guide, whom Legna has put in charge of our field trip today. Meet Ediug, our guide."

He welcomed them telepathically and stated what Angie had remembered Legna saying a very long time ago: "Now that you have met and communicated with me, you will recognize me. The more of us you meet, the more of us you will recognize. You won't have to remember our names or our physical appearance. Telepathically, you will know who we are." They exchanged mutual greetings.

"Earlier, we met your family and gave them a tour of the ship. They were fascinated and asked many questions," explained Ediug.

"Really?" questioned Angie. "We didn't even hear them leave the house. I guess we are a curious family." Everyone giggled.

Ediug continued. "There are many rooms on the ship with different purposes. This one is called the Astral Room, where the archangels meet with you in person."

He led the way. "Here is a Communications and Research Center where you can learn about various topics, including information on the colonization of the primitive planet. The lessons are taught and overseen by instructors giving you hands-on experience. On the astral plane, you gather information, and guides help answer your questions. However, there is much to be gained by in-person learning."

"Here is one of the favorite rooms that I know you have visited before, the Molecular Room where you dematerialize and your spirits entwine, resulting in a euphoric feeling. When you rematerialize, the two of you will have a deeper relationship. The Molecular Room will give you that total experience."

The collective consciousness was in total agreement, recalling this delightful interaction.

After a fascinating afternoon exploring the craft, the entourage headed back to the house. Sandalphon had left them at the airport, promising to return at nightfall. They would enjoy another visit to the backyard fairyland, followed by a visit to the gazebo and fireflies. This time Sandalphon would introduce them to the trees as well as providing accompanying music. For now, they would rest, freshen up, and enjoy another one of Wendy's home-cooked meals.

Time flew, and soon they heard music and knew that Sandalphon had returned. They greeted him and proceeded out the front door. Once again, Wendy circled the yard, lighting the Tiki torches, and then led them into the shed. The fairies danced around their shoulders to the delight of all.

Chapter 13 – Party Time with the Leprechauns, Fairies & Trees

Once again, the delightful aroma of breakfast woke up Angie, Andrew, Mary, and Matthew from a deep night's sleep. In a flash, they found themselves at the breakfast table, telling Wendy and the others about their visit to the spacecraft the day before. They quickly ate and got ready for another busy day, knowing that Sandalphon and Ariel would be arriving any minute.

A cheerful "Hello!" filled the air blending perfectly with the sounds of nature. Ariel had arrived, a vision of loveliness. She looked like a fairy princess dressed in a pale pink gown. Her crown of diamonds shimmered, reflecting the sunlight.

Angie jumped up and ran out on the porch to greet her, with the others following fast on her heels. "Ariel, we are so happy to see you and are looking forward to an adventurous day."

"I am happy to see you too. There you are, Wendy. The fairies that live on your property are thrilled and appreciate all you have done for them.

Wendy blushed as she responded, "I love the fairies too. I can remember seeing them in the yard when Angie and Mary were growing up. There were times when I accidentally stepped on a plant or messed up a fairy circle. They never got angry with me. I'm happy to be able to make it up to them now that I am in human form."

"Thank you, Wendy, on their behalf and my behalf as the Archangel of Nature."

The sounds of music filled the air. They turned to see Sandalphon with musical notes following him.

He greeted them. "Hello again. Before we go, I promised Archangel Michael that I would give you a message. The archangels have discussed what to call the new and old earth. The name 'earth' is necessary to describe the planet, so we have agreed to call it Earth II."

"We don't have to think about the ruination of the old earth any longer!" Matthew excitedly exclaimed. "This is excellent news." They all telepathically agreed, confirmed by the big smiles on their faces.

Ariel advised, "today will be a fun day filled with friends and merriment. Wendy and William will also be joining us. Sandalphon, please play us some beautiful melodies on your flute. Let's hold hands and transport part of the way there."

The entourage arrived on the roadway leading to the countryside with fields of four-leaf clovers as far as the eyes could see. Tall, stately trees surrounded hills and mounds. White cottages with thatched roofs dotted the landscape. At first glance, everything looked quiet and deserted. As Sandalphon's musical notes blanketed the area, the scene came to life. The trees shook their leaves and twisted their boughs as faces appeared on their trunks.

"The Trees!" exclaimed Angie as they waved to each other. Rapidly beating fairy wings filled the air as they flew in and around their guests. Leprechauns emerged and came running as fast as their little legs could take them. Their green suits and cornered hats contrasted with their orange hair. Some were blowing smoke rings from their pipes. Some held up a bottle in a toast to their visitors. Sandalphon was welcoming them with some Irish Folk Music.

"Top of the morning. Welcome to our community. I hope you can spend some time with us. We have a clearing rimmed with tables and chairs and encircled with garland. Let's meet there. We will get refreshments and our dancing shoes. Oh. My name is Paddy. Call me if you need anything. I'll gladly make it happen."

The guests made their way to the clearing. The Trees had moved to a space beyond the picnic area to ensure they could be part of the festivities and provide shade. Their branches were dripping with bright red apples. Green garland, decorated with colorful flowers, graced the pillars with fairies flitting among them.

Paddy returned shortly with his helpers carrying all types of liquid refreshments. His wife and daughter, Caitlin and Colleen, followed behind, carrying trays of food. The Trees seemed to bow when they saw apple pies set out on the tables.

A magnificent parade of fairies brought forth flower blooms of all colors, which they arranged as table centerpieces.

Archangel Ariel started the introductions. "Thank you, fairies, leprechauns, and the trees, for welcoming our friends. Please meet Angie, Andrew, Mary, Matthew, Wendy, and William. They helped save the loving souls shift to the Earth II."

"Cheers to you all!" said Paddy as he raised his bottle in a toast. Leprechauns raised their beverages, fairies bowed, and the trees rustled their leaves. A chorus of "Cheers!" rang out. The guests responded with their reciprocal toasts.

Sandalphon said two words that excited the group. "River Dance!" A dance team came forward, set up their lines, and started dancing. Leprechauns clapped in time to the music. Fairies grabbed their partners and flew above the group, dancing and joining in the rhythm. Even the Trees rustled their leaves in time to the music. The guests couldn't help but join in. It was an energetic dance festival that seemed to go on for hours. When the music finally stopped, everyone collapsed onto the ground to catch their breath and enjoy some beverages while giggles and laughter filled the air.

In unison, Caitlin and Coleen said, "apple pie," and started handing out plates of all sizes. There were small plates for the leprechauns and tiny button-sized dishes for the fairies. Guests received larger plates. The raucous group became quiet except for the smacking of lips and the clanging of spoons. The trees, pleased with themselves for providing perfect apples, rustled their branches.

Once again, Sandalphon announced, "River Dance!" Caitlin and Collen cleared the plates while the dance troupe retook the floor. The fairies grabbed their partners and, once again, flew above the group to join in. Clapping, knee-slapping, and spoon rapping accompanied the music. The trees shook their leaves and dropped some ruby red apples into the centerpiece baskets on the tables.

After what seemed like hours, the intensity of the festivities died down as the partygoers collapsed from exhaustion. Ariel announced, "It is evident that everyone thoroughly enjoyed themselves, and we thank you. However, it is time for us to take our leave."

Paddy started the traditional Irish blessing. Everyone joined in, repeating the lines in unison. "May the road rise up to meet you. May the wind be always at your back. May the sunshine warm upon your face, the rains fall soft upon your fields, and until we meet again, may God hold you in the palm of His hand." Those with beverages raised their glasses and bottles in a toast while others gave a thumbs up.

In response to this well-known blessing, Angie replied, "Thank you, our newfound friends. Until we meet again, may the angels keep you safe." The rest of the guests nodded in agreement.

They held hands and skipped down the road as Sandalphon led the way playing a lilting Irish jingle. When they were out of sight, they transported the rest of the way back home. They said their goodbyes to Sandalphon and Ariel. Exhausted from the day's events, they were sound asleep in no time.

Part II
New Worlds

Chapter 14 – Under the Sea with Legna

It had been a hectic couple of days. After a restful night and another delicious breakfast, Mary wanted to work with Wendy in the kitchen. William wanted to show Andrew and Matthew some projects he was working on. Angie decided to slip away and go to the beach.

Sitting on the warm sand, she found herself gazing out as far as her eyes could see. The waves were alive, gently lapping the shore. She decided to do a little wading. Sometimes fish would swim by tickling her toes. Dolphins broke the surface with their playful antics. Seashells, discarded by their occupants, washed ashore to the delight of collectors looking for that perfect specimen. *What lies beneath the vast oceans? What is hidden from view?* Those are the questions that had always intrigued Angie. She knew more about the universes full of planets and stars than she knew about the oceans right here on this planet, her native world. Countless times, she would sit on the beach and wonder, mesmerized by the sight and sounds of its majesty.

Archangel Michael was simultaneously sending them all welcoming news. Legna had a meeting with the governing body of one of the many underwater communities. He invited Angie, Mary, Andrew, and Matthew to accompany him. Angie's excitement was a challenge to her inquisitive nature. To say she was elated was an understatement.

There wasn't much time, so she dried off and ran back home, where she found the others getting ready to go. They said their good-byes or, as Wendy preferred to say, 'See you later' and were quickly on their way.

Archangel Michael had assembled the foursome in the Astral Room to wish them well. Angie blushed as Michael reminded her to keep her questions to a minimum. He asked Legna, who had joined them, to be gentle with Mary explaining her dislike of anything resembling an amusement park ride. As a fun aside, Michael suggested a food stop for Matthew. Andrew received his customary nod signifying that Michael wanted him to keep watch over his friends.

Wisps of clouds like angels' wings graced the skies as Archangel Michael wished them well.

"Thank you for giving us this opportunity," stated Angie. Archangel Michael nodded his head as he departed.

Legna stood in the middle of Angie and Mary with Andrew and Matthew on their loved ones' sides. They joined hands and transported to the observation deck inside a smaller flying saucer-type vehicle parked on Earth II's landing pad. Windows surrounded the entire deck. Crew members sat at computer screens mounted below windows offering the occupants a view to the universe and beyond.

Legna directed them to empty chairs, "You will occupy these seats for our voyage. Fasten your seat belts."

"Where are the keyboards?" asked Angie.

Legna replied, "Our computer equipment runs by thought."

"If I think of a command, will the computer react?" inquired Andrew.

"No," exclaimed Legna. "Imagine a fingerprint that activates your phone or another type of device. The computers are programmed to identify brain waves before they will accept any command. Are there any other questions before we begin?"

Timidly, Mary asked, "Will we be going very fast?"

In a calming and reassuring manner, Legna explained. "It will not seem very fast. I am confident you will enjoy the ride. You will not be frightened."

The others were genuinely concerned for Mary as they closely watched for her reaction. They were relieved when the worry lines disappeared from her face. A collective sigh of relief echoed throughout their consciousness.

Legna issued instructions to the crew and then announced. "In order for me to arrive on time for my meeting, we must go. Get comfortable and enjoy the view."

"Oh, look!" exclaimed Angie. William and Wendy were surrounded by the family and all waving goodbye in unison. They waved back from their seats aboard the craft.

Besides occasional oohs and ahhs, the only sound to be heard was a faint buzzing as the flying saucer took flight. The craft felt motionless as treetops whizzed by. The experience was like watching a movie on a big screen. Angie saw a smile creep across Mary's face and knew this was going to be a fantastic day.

The ship skimmed the water leaving the land and shoreline behind. The sunlight threw sparkles of glittering diamonds across the surface, kissing the ocean that gently rolled beneath them. The undulating waves added to their sense of calm. *It is beautiful, surreal.* Angie's thoughts were heard and shared by the others.

Angie had heard about the underwater colonies inhabited by aliens. Their homes had lots of picture windows, giving the illusion of living inside an aquarium.

Before long, they came upon a patchwork of small islands. Treetops appeared to grow right out of the water.

Legna explained, "This area is called Belau. The villagers oversee one of the most expansive coral reefs in the world. Belauns have visited the underwater colonies but never speak of them. It is our secret. We will not be meeting them or any earth dwellers on this visit. You may see some of them on the islands or waterways as we pass by.

No sooner had he made the statement, a sizeable handmade canoe glided across the water. It looked like a father and his sons were enjoying the ride on the turquoise lagoons.

Angie asked, "Will they see us? Can we wave?"

"They will not see us. Our privacy cloak is on. Any air disturbance will be considered the trade winds."

The small islands of treetops continued to rush past. Occasional waterfalls were spilling into calm pools of tropical blue waters. Before long, their sleek craft was skimming the wave tops of the open ocean. Prisms of sparkling light reflected off the surface.

In the distance, they could see a curious change on the ocean surface. There were no waves or whitecaps. The sea was as smooth as glass like a lake on a windless day.

As they stared straight ahead, wondering what they were observing, they heard Legna announce, "We are here. We will descend into the ocean depths."

"No. Please. You are going too fast! We will flip over!" A disturbing look of dread turned Mary's face a sickly green. Her knuckles were white with the intensity of her death grip. Angie thought Mary was about to cry or get sick or maybe both.

"Do not worry, Mary," consoled Legna. "Trust me. You will not feel the change. Your view is the only thing that will be different.

Leave the driving to me. Our ships have incredible maneuverability."

Before Mary could protest further, their craft gently tipped sideways as it separated the calm patch of the tropical blue ocean. It was as smooth as a knife cutting through softened butter. Prisms of bright colors surrounded them like a bounty of gems caught in the reflecting sunlight.

Angie observed the relief wash over Mary's face. They were heading down very gently. There was no discomfort; their ears did not pop. With ease, the picture on the window-like screens in front of them had changed from a bright blue cloudless sky to a turquoise, diamond-studded ocean. They slipped into the depths with the precision of a hi-diving champion, barely leaving a splash.

Chapter 15 – Bubble Magic

Towers of kelp appeared before them, gently undulating in the currents. The reflections turned this otherwise brown forest a verdant shade of emerald green. Their craft moved gracefully, gently bumping the lush, dense growth out of the way. Occasionally colorful fish swam by. Angie thought kelp was supposed to be murky and dismal compared to the beautiful shade of green she was observing.

Legna assumed his role as a tour guide and announced, "These kelp fields hide and protect the colony from view. Divers would not expect to find a coral reef so far below or so far from the islands or a shoreline. Coral likes sunlight and does not flourish beyond sixty feet. We will travel down about fifty feet. This depth is adequate to keep unwanted visitors away while providing a beautiful environment for the colony."

The kelp fields thinned out, revealing schools of tropical fish gliding past them. Appearing out of the blue was a glass structure. As large as a great room, each window was circular, giving the illusion of large bubbles. At times, they would glimpse some interior movement. Upon more careful examination, they could see the occupants going about their business. The bubbles sat atop a lush, vibrant coral reef, a breathtaking sight. The guests were speechless.

The vivid colors and graceful movements hid the fact that they had reached their destination. Unbeknownst to them, the craft had effortlessly set down on a landing pad. A glass door opened, they drove in, and the water drained from the enclosure. They had arrived.

"Couldn't we have transported here?" timidly asked Mary.

"Absolutely," confirmed Legna. However, you would have missed the views and the experience of the journey. It wasn't too bad, was it?"

Mary smiled as she admitted, "It wasn't scary at all, and I would have hated to miss it. Thank you for the experience and for being patient with me."

Legna proceeded saying, "There is another reason. I wanted you to understand the workings of this colony. Most of our underwater dwellers do transport here. Their goods and supplies arrive through this entry point. Let's go in and do a tour before my appointment with the Eungem governing body."

Angie asked, "Will we be able to speak to anyone? What language do they speak here?"

"Angie, don't worry. Everyone communicates through thought."

A spacecraft door opened, and steps materialized before them. They followed Legna across the landing pad to a door that led to a warehouse. Goods lined the shelves like obedient soldiers. Crates and boxes were neatly stacked everywhere, hiding their contents from view.

"This is the industrial center of the community," explained Legna continuing in his position as a tour guide.

They ventured through another door and found themselves inside an aquarium. A glass bubble encircled three-quarters of the reception area. They rushed to the glass in time to see schools of yellow fish dutifully following their leader. Soon, another progression of fish in iridescent shades of blue swam by. A couple of dolphins touched their noses to the glass, greeting the newcomers. Sharks swam by, seemingly oblivious to the onlookers. Beautiful coral peeked from beneath the undulating grasses that seemed to wave to them. The guests were mesmerized, lost in the underwater paradise.

"Come," instructed Legna. "We are short on time. You may observe the aquatic activity later."

He ushered them over to the reception desk. "Hcar, these are my guests. Thank you for inviting them to visit your family. I will meet you later in your home." And with those parting words, Legna was gone.

Hcar was much smaller than Legna. He looked like the aliens from Area 52 on Earth I. "Welcome to our colony, which we call Eungem. It means 'below' in the Palauan language. Our first stop will be to visit with my family. Please, follow me."

They exited the reception area and ventured down a long hallway where more corridors branched out to the right and left and straight ahead. They followed their guide, Hcar, who entered a doorway at the very end. A couple of anxious youth rushed to greet them. They looked just like Hcar but smaller. Angie could not guess who was a male or female from their outward appearance. However, she could tell by their thoughts.

"Hello. You must be our guests. Come see our home." The young ones pulled them toward their cute, cozy bedrooms. *There are no windows.* Angie thought. *But that makes perfect sense because bedrooms are for sleeping, and I doubt I could sleep if I had the option to gaze at the ocean's beauty.*

Giggles erupted as Angie realized they had read her musings. She found herself laughing too. The children practically dragged them back to the main room. Beautiful ocean views surrounded them. They were inside the bubbles they had observed from the craft. Strategically positioned seating in front of the aquarium windows enhanced the viewing enjoyment. Angie thought that this was precisely the way she would have designed it.

"Your home is beautiful," she exclaimed. "You are so lucky to live down here."

"Yes, we are," agreed Hcar. "Come. My wife has prepared a meal for you. We do not require food for nourishment. However, we find the practice of consuming very enjoyable."

"Us too!" offered Matthew without hesitation. "On Earth II, we get all our nourishment from the drinking water. However, we enjoy eating for the fun of it too. Our food is plant-based."

"We too get our nourishment from the drinking water which is purified seawater," explained Hcar. "Try some."

Mary politely commented, "This is delicious. Thank you. It is a little different from our reservoir water, which is also tasty. You must come to visit and try our water someday."

They took their places at the table. It was no surprise that all chairs faced the windows, affording them breathtaking aquatic views.

Hcar explained. "On this beautiful planet, the plentiful fish are responsible for our nutrient-dense water. The fish and shellfish perform specific functions to preserve our environment, especially the reef. The Mangrove crabs are the janitors. We need all aquatic life for their contribution, not for food."

Hcar's wife entered with several serving dishes. Matthew was ready to stop the friendly conversation and asked, "What have we here?"

"This is my wife, Zcar. Please tell us what you have put before us, my dear."

"We have a seaweed salad and a soil-grown salad. Lettuce, tomatoes, radishes, seeds, and much more are grown in our greenhouses. Although plentiful, our seaweed has many functions, and consuming it is considered a delicacy for special occasions. Welcome to our home and table. Enjoy!"

Mary joined in on the conversation, "Angie and I love preparing food. Perhaps someday you could visit us and sample some of the dishes that we would be delighted to prepare for you. We could exchange recipes, and you could taste our water."

"Thank you. Perhaps someday we will have that opportunity," replied Zcar as the children echoed a chorus of "Can we? Please."

The room fell silent except for the passing of bowls and the clinking of utensils. When conversation resumed, it was full of praise and admiration of the exquisite offerings.

Chapter 16 – Aquarium Auditorium

They laid down their utensils and napkins. The guests and hosts sat back and turned their attention toward the windows and the natural beauty before them.

Legna returned from his meeting and asked, "Have you had time to enjoy the view? Hcar, have you explained the aquatic life?"

"I was just going to. Please enjoy some delicacies that Zcar has prepared?"

Hcar took on the air of a college professor imparting wisdom to his listeners. "The pressure at this depth is extreme. Our windows are stronger than any windows known to man. Our interactions with aquatic life are varied. The dolphins communicate with us, the sharks ignore us, and the Manta Rays delight us with their graceful angel wings. The parrotfish, with their beaks, break down the old corals making room for new growth. Eels will pop straight up when the water is calm. There are many different types of jellies that no longer need protective stingers."

Legna added, "The Eungems monitor and assist all aquatic life. The ban on mining and harvesting is essential for its preservation."

Hcar carried the idea further. "This protected area gives us a perfect place to live and study the underwater environment. When we must leave our community's confines, we have a specially designed wetsuit that mimics fish gills. There is no need for air tanks."

"Can you please tell us more about how you can go underwater without tanks?" asked Andrew.

"Oh my gosh! A mermaid!" Mary nearly fell off her chair as she jumped up to point out her newfound discovery.

Hcar chuckled and said, "Perfect timing. That is not a mermaid but one of us. Our diving gear is customized. It is like a wet suit but has one tail fin allowing for extremely powerful propulsion and steering. The fin also acts as a formidable tool to move unwanted items and nudge the larger fish out of the way."

"How do they breathe?" the group asked telepathically.

"It is quite resourceful. Like the dolphins, we have elastic lungs that can expand to hold a large quantity of oxygen. The hood of the wet suit has specifically designed with gills over the mouth area. Water enters the suit, but only oxygen is permitted to enter the mouth and lungs. Everything else is expelled back out of the gills."

"That is ingenious," remarked Andrew.

Hcar and Legna let them observe the 'mermaid' for a few minutes before Andrew asked, "How do you get the energy you need down here at these depths?"

Hcar continued, "Have you heard of the trenches? The most popular is the Mariana Trench. The Yap Trench is closer. These trenches are the convergence of the tectonic plates where steam, light, and minerals escape from the earth's depths. We have learned how to harness this energy through large underwater pipes. Surface sunlight is captured and stored using solar panels that float beneath the surface. They are monitored and moved to avoid detection."

"We saw a patch of water that was unusually still before we descended. Is that caused by the solar panels perhaps calming the wave action?" Andrew questioned.

"Yes," replied Hcar. "That is exactly why you saw the calm patch in the ocean."

"How can the pipes separate the steam from the minerals?" continued Andrew.

"That is quite simple. Water carries minerals, which are denser than the air. One pipe pulls in both, and then a lower pipe takes the mineral water, and the upper pipe takes the steam. Both go into storage vats where they are processed."

Legna interrupted the lesson. "Hcar, thank you, but we must go. We will leave our hosts allowing Hcar to get back to the reception area and allow his family to resume their activities, including some schooling for the youngsters. Thank you, Hcar, and your family for the kind hospitality you have extended to our visitors."

"Yes, thank you. Where are we going next?" Angie politely asked.

Legna replied, "We are going to the great hall where the residents gather for serious meetings as well as enjoyable activities. The Great Hall is where I met the Eungem governing body earlier today. Surprises are waiting for us there."

"Surprises? Will we walk, or will we transport?" Angie enthusiastically inquired.

"We will transport to avoid interrupting the lives of the residents. Please hold hands and come with me," Legna instructed.

They found themselves at the back of a large, empty auditorium with perfectly arranged theater seats. Legna told someone, "Open the anti-distraction curtain now."

They looked up to see massive, dark blue draperies parting as they swayed to either side, revealing a window to the aquatic life beyond. Without waiting for permission, the group rushed down the ramp, unsteady on their feet, while negotiating the decline. With mouths agape, they maintained total silence. Their heads rotated this way and that, like you would see at a tennis match, as sea creatures came into view. Soon the silence was broken by oohs and ahhs, complete with finger-pointing. Lines of colorful fish were playing follow the leader.

Mary was the first to comment, "Look at the cute seahorses hiding amid the coral. Some are drifting while others anchor in place with their tails."

A turtle came into view gracefully propelled by his powerful flippers, and dolphins nodded their heads. They observed the parrotfish that Hcar had pointed out. They recognized some shark varieties by the dorsal fins. Lost in thought and amazement, one by one, they snapped back to reality and turned toward their guide.

Chapter 17 – Ocean Depths:
Featuring Archangel Manakel

Unbeknownst to the aquatic observers, members of the Eungem community had filled the auditorium behind them. Hcar and his family were seated upfront and received subtle finger waves from their dinner guests when they realized they had company.

Legna pointed to the chairs. "Please sit." The designers had arranged the seating for optimum aquatic viewing enjoyment. He took a position in front of them. "Welcome to everyone. This meeting is for our guests from Earth II. We hope all of you will enjoy it." He turned his focus toward Angie, Mary, Andrew, and Matthew. "Throughout your journeys, you have met many archangels, with unique powers and dominion over different areas. It is almost time for you to meet an archangel who has dominion over the oceans. But first, I have asked some old friends to join us."

"Hello!" Ariel announced in her cheerful voice that seemed to reverberate around the room in a series of unending echoes. She glided in, a vision of loveliness befitting the backdrop of the tropical waters

Her old friends could hardly get out of their chairs fast enough as they made a mad dash to welcome her.

Legna patiently waited for Ariel and the guests to exchange greetings before asking them to return to their seats.

In a voice that was as gentle as a breeze, she continued, "It is so nice to see everyone. Thank you for the warm welcome. For those that have not met me before, I am Ariel, the nature angel, the Archangel of the Outdoors. My job is to ensure everyone treats every creature with respect, from the smallest to the largest. I also must remind everyone that they must do everything in their power to preserve the earth."

Applause rang out. Legna stood, and the room fell silent, allowing Ariel to continue.

"Thank you for all your efforts to save the loving souls and help them transport to earth's replacement planet. We must all work together to keep Earth II in balance for the benefit of all its inhabitants. It is time for a visit from another old friend, Archangel Haniel."

Haniel lit up the room like a moonbeam on a clear night. Her aura and body were in shades of pale blue depicting a full moon, high in the sky with a lunar halo encircling her head. She appeared like a dainty vision of elegant loveliness while emanating a powerful, formidable vibration.

"Greetings." My name is Archangel Haniel. I am the Archangel of Intuition, and I help everyone understand and accept themselves and others."

Mary was the first to lead the welcome procession, yearning for an archangel hug. Mary loved Haniel and wished she could be more assertive on the inside of her meek exterior. This formidable archangel commanded peace and love.

Once the foursome returned to their seats, Haniel said. "Thank you, Ariel and Legna, for inviting me to your gathering. I work closely with the moon controlling the tides. It is always a thrill to visit these glass palaces beneath the sea. I'm delighted you invited these guests to visit this amazing place and community."

Haniel continued by saying, "To fully understand the ocean deep, there is an archangel that we would like to introduce. His name is Manakel. He has dominion over the oceans."

Manakel glided in. His robe was the color of the crystal-clear blue patch they had observed upon their arrival. Whitecaps hemmed his gown, cresting and then disappearing like the waves mightily approaching the shoreline before calming down to peaceful lapping. His wings were feathery, unpredictably lapping at the air. His halo was reminiscent of the sparkling gems that had descended with them into the ocean depths. His sleeves, slightly hidden from view by his enormous wings, seemed to usher forth schools of fish, alternating between tropical to massive sea creatures. In his hand, he held a staff adorned with carvings of sea life.

"Hello. My name is Manakel. I sense that you are fascinated by my wardrobe and may have properly figured out that I am the protector of all aquatic life. My main function is achieving balance. We no longer have the predatory cycle on Earth II because the water's nutrients sustain all life. However, it is often necessary to encourage the larger fish to move to a new location allowing sufficient room for the smaller ones. With the help of my mighty staff, I guide the mammals, fish, and plant life that dwell in the sea."

"Amazing," thought Angie. *"I never thought of that before."* When Angie heard Hcar's children giggle, she realized that everyone had listened to her thoughts. She smiled and cleared her mind.

Without missing a beat, Manakel resumed his speech. "I have helped Legna and his people find ideal places for their colonies. Their presence beneath the sea is essential as the watchers of many underground paradises. The people of Palau tend to the coral reefs.

"I am also known as the angel of knowledge of good and evil. I bring stability, confidence, and harmony and take away fears and negative emotions by transforming them into positive ones. These tasks are essential in the vast ocean with sharks and whales down to the minute creatures that the eye cannot see. There must always be a balance. I work with Ariel with her command over the non-sea creatures, such as the birds. I work with Haniel, who has command over the moon, which affects the tides. Together we achieve perfect harmony.

"The new planet, Tenalp, is not plant-based. The creatures on land and sea are predatory. Humans will require food and will hunt, prepare, and consume fish, animals, and plant life. My task will be markedly similar to Earth I. It is a challenge to achieve stability within the cycle of life. Humans will have to learn primitive survival skills. The three of us will be spending much time on Tenalp to achieve the perfect balance among the rapidly changing landscape."

Legna stepped forward and with the wave of his hand, encouraged Ariel and Haniel to join Manakel back on stage. Their audience erupted in applause, and with of flutter of their wings, the Archangels departed.

Angie was nearly speechless as "*Wow!*" escaped her thoughts. Legna thanked the Eungems, who had started to file out of the auditorium. Legna motioned to the remaining foursome to join him on the platform. They joined hands, not sure where they were going. In an instant, Legna returned them to the Meet-and-Greet area on the astral plane. Matthew made a beeline for the dining area. Mary ran over to the unicorns. Angie and Andrew thanked Legna, who acknowledged their appreciation.

"Legna?" asked Andrew. "What happened to the aircraft that brought us here?"

"I had one of the crew transport over to return it to the airfield. Thank you for your concern."

Angie was still lost in her thoughts of a fabulous day and could only articulate "Wow" as she melted into Andrew's arms. Together they collapsed onto the grassy fields, still locked in their embrace. That was Legna's cue to depart.

Chapter 18 – Stars Amid the Cosmos:
Featuring Archangel Orion

While everyone was daydreaming about their recent underwater adventure, Archangel Michael suddenly appeared, startling them back to the present.

"Thank you!" Angie blurted out. "Everything was wonderful. We loved every moment."

"I am delighted you enjoyed yourselves. Let's go over to the gazebo where you can sit," Michael replied.

Gazebo? As they turned, there it was. Angie's startled expression revealed her momentary surprise. Then she smiled. *We are with the mightiest of the Archangels. If he wants a gazebo, no problem, he can conjure one up.* The gazebo was pure white complete with sturdy benches topped with elegant, tufted cushions. Since they had chosen to remain in their earthly bodies, they appreciated the comfort. Fresh flowers of all shapes and sizes cascaded like waterfalls from intricate latticework. The flowers came alive with their smiling faces bobbing and swaying in the breezes. The mingled scents of this floral bouquet delightfully tickled their noses.

Michael stood in the enormous entry and announced, "It is now time for some of the lost souls to relocate to Tenalp to work on their karma. The mission is massive. Your task is to watch over the new arrivals, but you will not be working alone. It is time to meet my Archangel of the Universe, who has dominion over the multitude of planets and solar systems out to the farthest reaches of the galaxies.

"His name is Orion. He has command over the constellation by the same name. His portal is the middle star in Orion's belt through which he broadcasts his healing light and frequency. Visualize the imaginary character Superman who encircles the earth and travels throughout the universe. After you meet Orion, you will be able to envision him in Superman's place."

Michael read their minds and saw images of Superman zooming this way and that. After a brief pause, he continued, "Orion can also see every facet of the entire universe. To achieve harmony and balance, he is skilled at rapidly fitting all the pieces together like a giant jigsaw puzzle."

The imagery was working, so Michael continued, "Orion is 'faster than a speeding bullet,' to borrow an earthly phrase. Conversely, he encourages everyone to slow down. Human beings have a lesser frequency and need to see the big picture at a much slower vibration. Please welcome the galactic Archangel, Orion, the Archangel of the Cosmos, your guide through the celestial realms."

Orion drifted onto the scene with twinkling stars cascading all around him. The group was momentarily blinded and dazed.

A new pleasant fragrance had filled the gazebo. Following the scent upward, the flowers had changed to beautiful night-blooming Moonflowers. The kind that opens at dusk and closes during daylight. While open, they infuse the night air with their pleasant aroma. The white-pink blossoms looked like full moons among Orion's starlight.

Orion wore a robe made of exquisite midnight blue velvet. The fabric's folds swayed on the gentle breezes that danced through the gazebo, sending reflections of thousands of shimmering stars radiating in all directions. The stars swirled around like a snow globe set in motion. Amid the dazzling light show, Orion wore a star-studded crown.

Andrew stepped forward and offered a welcome. "We are privileged to meet you and look forward to working with you."

"Thank you. Glad to meet you as well," Orion replied as he approached the gathering and offered archangel hugs amid the starlight. The shared consciousness of the group felt his love radiating throughout the universe.

"You will be our Star Archangel," offered Angie. We have cherished names for some of you, like Raziel, our Rainbow Archangel.

"I feel like I already know you. I watched over the success of your mission to save the loving souls. Thank you. As for me, I like to think of myself as playful, like Peter Pan of the galaxies, flying here and there. I know you were wondering why we have not met before. I was busy working among the stars. However, Michael has included me in the mission to colonize Tenalp. Now that I am needed there, you will see me often."

Angie's thoughts had become loud and clear. *Are we going to fly around with Orion? What exactly will we be doing? Why does he fly around the universe when he can transport there?*

Michael responded to Angie's shared thoughts. "The details of the mission are being worked out and will be explained in due time. Orion, please elaborate on why you fly throughout the universe?"

Orion nodded toward Michael. "You are correct. I can instantly transport anywhere. The universe consists of comets, asteroids, black holes, and space debris, and so much more. Let's not forget that each star represents a soul. As I fly around and pass the soul stars, I beam love, light, and healing along the way. Archangel

Michael, do I have time to take them for a spin around the universe?"

Mary turned pale as a lump rose in her throat. She grabbed Matthew's and Andrew's arms in a death grip. *I must do this for the sake of the mission. I must!*

Archangel Orion sensed her hesitation and said, "Mary, do not worry. We won't go too fast. Your fear of flight originated after years of living within the earth's gravitational pull. True happiness lies in the non-physical and beyond. Let go of your feelings and enjoy the ride."

Mary anchored herself to her companions in a white-knuckle grip as they gently lifted off. They soared upwards and found themselves on top of puffy clouds. While Mary was still skittish, she had to admit she was no longer terrified. She would not and could not look down. The others enjoyed the show, identifying coastlines, mountains, and ice caps.

Gently they continued, gliding past an asteroid and riding alongside a comet. The group felt like they were part of a celestial fireworks display. The stars twinkled as they passed by, emitting love from their souls. They traveled past planets, moons, and soon they encircled beloved Pluto and headed back. Another comet streaked by, leaving a brilliant trail that rivaled Orion's star show. Up close, the rings of Saturn were beautiful, spinning like a gyroscope. The massive size of Jupiter was daunting. They all instantly recognized planet earth and took a spin around it before their ride came to an end.

Back in the gazebo, Andrew admitted, "I am in awe of the world, of the universe we live in, of every minute detail. Thank you for opening our eyes, freeing us from our worldly thoughts." A sense of humility pervaded the group of friends.

Orion personally addressed Mary. "You seem at peace, Mary. Did you enjoy the ride?"

"Oh, yes! Thank you for taking it slow. I felt like an eagle soaring above the clouds. Thank you."

Orion continued, "You are very welcome. Now all of you can see the universe from a different perspective. You can explain to others that when a small detail on the pages of life goes awry, it is minor compared to the broader picture. Our life's purpose is part of the universal book of love. We cannot get distracted by the minor imbalances along the way."

Archangel Michael asked, "Orion, will you summarize your task on the primitive planet?"

"Sure," Orion agreed. "We will help souls colonize in small groups without the benefits of mass communication. Fear will strike at their hearts as they experience hardships. I will help them find peace while helping them discover their full potential. We will explain our methods in further detail with the help of other Archangels you will meet on this mission."

"What about their guardian angels?" questioned Angie.

Orion replied, "Angie, that is an excellent question. Guardian angels are responsible for helping specific souls. Although Archangels can help them individually, our power can extend to an entire group, planet, and universe. I can help them see the bigger picture, which is essential to colonize this planet.

"May I please ask one more question?" Without waiting for approval, Angie continued, "when we see rainbows, we think of Archangel Raziel. When we see an eclipse or shooting stars, is that you?"

"Yes. It is my way to encourage mortal souls to expand their vision. It helps them realize they are not alone, not an accident of creation. When they look up, they can visualize the bigger picture, so much more than mere humans. This realization heightens their vibrational level."

Archangel Michael stepped forward. "Thank you, Orion. Will you stay while I introduce our next guest?"

"Absolutely," Archangel Orion agreed. "And, to my new friends and assistants in this next mission, anytime you need me, envision yourselves enveloped by thousands of stars. I will see you shining brightly and come to your side."

Chapter 19 – Truth & Justice:
Featuring Archangel Mariel

Archangel Orion stepped back as Michael took center stage. "Before we discuss ways to colonize the planet, let's get to know those who will occupy it. The Archangel who knows them intimately is Archangel Mariel. He is arriving now."

They followed Michael's gaze toward a sunset. Brushstrokes of magenta accentuated the pale blue sky. Iridescent hues reached out to paint the gazebo in matching colors. In the middle of the color pallet, a dazzling figure glided into view. His shimmering robe swirled and danced in concert with Orion's stars. Blue flames encased in sparklers radiated in all directions encircling his head. As the group gazed wide-eyed, Angie reflected, *Can there be anything more beautiful than a sunrise and a sunset.*

Angie, overcome with gratitude, commented, "We have met many amazing Archangels, and just when you think you could not meet another who could take your breath away, you introduce us to more. We are so privileged."

Magenta pink pansies magically transformed the garland that ringed the gazebo. Orion's stars bounced around the nodding heads of hundreds of these colorful flowers, creating a halo effect.

Mary added, "I feel like I am dreaming. Everything is beautiful, thrilling, and beyond belief."

Without a word, this magnificent Archangel opened his wings. They dreamily meandered forward into his welcoming, powerful embrace. He kissed them on the forehead, followed by a kiss on the top of their heads.

"Why did you kiss our foreheads and our heads?" asked Angie.

"Your third eye chakra is located in the middle of your forehead. All meaningful kisses invoke a sense of enlightenment deep inside of you. A kiss on the lips signifies love, while a kiss on the forehead speaks to the highest realms of your spirit. A kiss on the top of your head speaks to your soul.

"My name is Mariel, and I connect to the chakra known as the soul star. There are energy centers, known as chakras, for every part of the body. The common ones are the root, heart, throat, third eye, and crown. The soul star chakra is the seat of your soul, located above your head, and is a direct connection to your higher self. It holds all the information about your Akashic records, karmic past, and past lives."

Angie, appearing to look above everyone's heads for the soul chakra, asked, "When we clear our chakras, is our soul star included in that process?"

"That is an excellent question," replied Mariel. "The answer is yes. All chakras are cleared even if you are only focusing on certain ones."

Mariel continued, "My pink color signifies the highest and purest intent of the heart. The blue flame holds the power of manifestation."

He turned to look over his shoulder at the other Archangels who had retreated, making room for him.

"Hello, my dear friend, Orion. As always, I look forward to working alongside you."

"As do I," Orion agreed.

"Hello, Michael. Thank you for allowing me to explain my role and meet my assistants. I have witnessed them from afar, and I'm anxious to get to know them better."

Michael replied, "it is our pleasure to have you visit us. Please proceed."

"As you are aware," explained Mariel, "all Archangels have their areas of expertise, and mine is truth and justice. I fight for the love and healing of humanity. As the Archangel of Memories, I know every single one of the first wave of incarnates. We met, reviewed their prior lifetimes, and created realistic karmic restoration plans. These souls went through a battery of tests and had their plans challenged. Only when I felt they were ready did I recommend their reincarnation to a select board of Archangels. Their lifespans will be short, allowing them to return to the astral plane to review their progress and make necessary adjustments to their future plans."

Archangel Michael interjected, "Archangel Zadkiel took the group on a virtual trip to witness the final days of planet earth, which they had not seen before.

"Excellent. Seeing is believing, making my task easier. My job is not as exciting as Orion flying around the universe or Manakel with the beautiful vast oceans. My important task is to keep the souls on their loving paths. They will not remember me or their plans to heal their karma. I need your help to observe and identify souls in need of assistance."

Mariel proceeded. "Our help must be gentle. Feelings of remorse may unknowingly surface, and a sense of dread could suffocate them. That is when I bring them love and mercy by nudging them along the loving path. Repentant souls could find it difficult to forgive themselves, remembering the pain they inflicted on others. We mustn't permit that to happen.

"I like Archangel Michael's use of imagery," Mariel said. "Let's take a peek at what it is like on Tenalp."

A screen appeared before them. The group watched whitecaps on top of the vast expanse of the clear blue ocean, seeming to smile and greet them. The waves traveled to lap the sandy shoreline sprinkled with perfect seashell specimens. Moving inland, a scalloped topography of treetops, like pom-poms pulsating in encouragement, cheered their arrival.

"Looks like Paradise," Mariel continued. "On Earth, you would expect to find a resort around the corner. Let's go in closer and take a look at the living conditions."

They followed a beam of sunlight to a clearing in the forest. The partially obscured light cast a patchwork of shadows on the bare earth below. Dirty-looking people were rinsing crude garments in a stream while others were spearing fish. Partially dressed, children were running around gleefully chasing one another.

Mariel narrated the scene. "You can see that there is no fire to cook their fish. They eat it raw. Fortunately, pollutants have not spoiled the lands and tributaries. Notice the bushes laden with fruit, a mainstay in their limited diet. They have realized that plants drop their seeds and new plants grow, so now you will observe some simple gardening. See that cave over there? That is where they sleep and seek shelter. It is dark, damp, and bone-chilling. For their safety, they do not venture out before sunup and quickly retreat by the time the sunsets."

Angie commented, "We have enjoyed so many modern conveniences. Even if we try to imagine a life without electricity and fire, I don't believe we could ever envision a life this basic."

Mariel resumed his narration. "This is how it was at the beginning of all civilizations when their main focus was on survival. The new occupants of Tenalp will have much time to think while waiting for the morning light. That is when I work my magic, so to speak."

Archangel Michael added, "Archangel Mariel is the master of disbursing loving thoughts."

Mariel agreed, "Yes. It can be a challenge. Deep in the recesses of their souls, among their suppressed memories, they instinctively know, although not consciously, what kind of choices they must make. When a situation presents itself, I nudge them toward love and mercy. For instance, when a child cries, I nudge them toward compassion. When someone gets injured, I urge them to nurture. When they witness a solitary soul, I help them yearn for companionship. And so it goes. When the other group members see a loving gesture, they will learn to react in kind. They must learn to stand up for what's right and loving."

Mariel continued, "We can give them a little nudge, emphasizing 'little.' They must learn that a loving reaction feels good. The more varied the experiences are, the better. They will feel the terror of severe weather such as a hurricane. Crops will wither from the heat, and streams will dry up. They will work together to survive. On the other hand, they will have reasons to celebrate, to share in a feast, or rejoice in the birth of a child. Music and dancing will help bring souls together."

Their glimpse of Tenalp ended, and Archangel Michael stepped forward and announced, "Orion and Mariel will be leaving us."

They bid each other farewell with promises of working together very soon. The gazebo returned to its white, flowerless state.

"It is time for Legna to take you to his craft. I will meet you onboard from time to time, as well as on the surface. Until then, I bid you a peaceful night's rest."

Legna appeared and took Archangel Michael's place before them. He gestured for them to hold hands for their trip to the spacecraft.

Chapter 20 – On Board a UFO

Once onboard, they went straight to their sleeping chambers.

A crew member appeared with a food tray. "Legna thought you might enjoy some refreshments before you settled in for the night."

"Yes. Thank you," piped up Matthew, with the others nodding in agreement.

"Fresh strawberries with some chocolate! Yum!" announced Angie.

"Pizza," shouted Matthew. "Let's dig in."

Before long, they had their fill and turned in for the night.

The following morning, Legna appeared on the scene. "Since this will be your home away from home, I would like you to become familiar with this craft. It's brand new with many upgrades.

"I thought we knew the best places—the Observation Deck, our Sleeping Quarters, and, of course, the Molecular Room," stated Angie.

"Follow me, and I'll show you to other areas you are welcome to use and enjoy."

"Here is the Communication and Research Center. We will show you how to use the devices later so you may access them at will."

"So, we will have access to your computers?" asked Andrew.

"In a manner of speaking," explained Legna. "We will assemble for an information session after the tour. Follow me."

"Enter here, and you will find our Hydroponic Growing Center. Please meet Tae. I'll leave you with him so he can show you around."

Tae welcomed them and explained, "Some of our food is grown on the ship, reducing the need for storage. The walls and planters are composed of a thin crystal material. They provide the light needed for growth but not too bright to dry out the soil. The nutrient-rich water circulates through the hydroponic system. Fans circulate the air for pollination."

"Do you also synthesize food?" asked Andrew

"Yes, we do, and we can replicate the original taste and texture. Adding some freshly grown herbs and tasty garnishes further enhances its flavor."

Legna returned and thanked Tae. He directed the group to another room. "This is our Nutrition Area, what you would call a kitchen. Please meet our top chef, Laem. He will introduce you to the refrigeration, storage, and cooking conveyances."

"Hello, and welcome to my domain! I'm happy to show you around. I understand that you like to cook and eat. I already know some of your favorites, as you know from the treats I had sent over to you last night. As Tae explained, we synthesize some ingredients and gather others from our growing area."

"I don't see anything to cook with," observed Mary.

Onboard a craft, we must utilize every space, and we must secure everything. Travel is typically very smooth, but occasionally an anomaly will give us a tilt or jolt." Laem stepped toward two adjoining cabinet doors and pulled on the handles. Accordion-type cabinetry shelves unfolded, revealing storage and a full pantry.

"Wow!" the foursome echoed.

"I would love to have kitchen storage like this," added Angie. "What about a dining area?"

"Good question and you are standing on it." Laem closed the cabinet doors and asked them to step back. He tapped his toe on a rectangular shape on the floor, and a tabletop rose to a perfect height.

"Amazing!" marveled Angie. "What about chairs?"

"We do not use chairs in here. We spend too much time sitting, so when it is time to eat, we like to move freely around the table, similar to a buffet, and when your plate is full, you stop wherever you are and eat. The rotating serving dishes make the food convenient for all. It is quite enjoyable once you get used to it. Or you may eat in the Multipurpose Room where you will find tables and chairs. I prepared some breakfast sandwiches for you with some fresh juice. Enjoy."

"These are delicious!" mumbled Matthew with a mouth full. The others nodded while they continued to eat and drink.

"It is time to move on," announced Legna, who had entered the area.

Laem extended an invitation. "You are welcome to come back at any time, including joining us for meals. I enjoyed showing you around and hope to see you again soon."

"Thank you so very much," responded Angie. "The tour was fascinating."

"I'd love to have some of your recipes," requested Mary.

"The food is delicious. I'm sure we will join you again soon," confirmed Matthew.

Legna led them down a hallway and stopped in front of an area that looked like a small elevator. "Below are our crew quarters. The crew member steps on the platform, and his weight moves it down. When he steps off of it, it comes back up. Be careful if you come across an opening without the pad. That would mean it is in use."

Andrew asked, "what happens if you are down there and want to come back up?"

"There is a call button to lower the pad," explained Legna.

Legna stopped at the next area and invited them in. "This is our Multipurpose Room. It is a dedicated space for the crew, family, and guests." Pointing to desks, he continued, "those are computer stations where you can view distant lands, listen to music or do some research."

"How do the computers work?" asked Andrew.

"I'll show you later when we return to the Communication and Research Center. First, we have some other rooms to visit. This next room is called the Astral Room. It is a space where the Archangels come to meet with us."

After they looked around, Legna suggested, "Let's return to your sleeping quarters. The tour is far from over, but there are a few things I want to show you.

Once they arrived, Legna continued, "When not in use, the air is removed from the mattresses and pillows, making them extremely flat for space-saving storage. Please observe."

Legna removed a flat item from a storage area. It looked like a thin blanket or sheet. He attached a device to it, and it expanded into the size of a double mattress! He proceeded to do the same with a pillow while he explained, "The fabric is a material that will hold in or keep out the air, and yet it is very comfortable for sleeping."

He then proceeded to re-attach the device and remove the air from a pillow. It flattened out. "Did you know that you have been sleeping on these very same types of pillows and mattresses?"

The group shook their heads *no* as they stared in amazement.

"Now, follow me to the observation deck."

They obediently followed, wondering what would be different.

Legna pointed as he said, "Notice our chairs. They swivel and have gyroscope bases that are unaffected by the tilting or rotating of the ship. The crew can swing their chairs around to join a meeting and then swing back to their instrument panels."

"I don't see any instruments or panels. I just see lots of little squares or buttons," observed Andrew.

"Yes, and those buttons are toggles. Here. Push this one." A screen enlarged before them, displaying altitude and temperature readings. "Now, press it again." Andrew did, and the display disappeared. "This is a new ship with many space-saving advances. The display screen will automatically enlarge if something is not registering within the expected parameters."

Legna continued the tour. "These are the craft's Cleansing Rooms. A waterless mist cleans every pore of your body and every strand of your hair. It only takes a matter of seconds. You don't get wet, so you don't need a towel. You don't even need to remove your clothes. There is no soap, no washcloths, and no Loofah sponges. It is a unique but thoroughly enjoyable experience. You may use them many times during the same day.

"Our drinking and cooking water is synthesized and nutrient-dense. We only use what we require at any given time to avoid the need for storage.

"Now. Please follow me to the area you have all been anxious to visit, The Communication and Research Center.

There were workstations lined up like desks in a classroom with a lecturer's podium at the head. There were more of the swivel-type chairs but no keyboards.

Angie, observing crystals on the worktables that were in the shape of pyramids, asked, "What are those?"

"Scientifically speaking, they are six-sided Pyramidal Crystals. We refer to them as Eyes. Technically they are Interspatial Interactive Information stations or Triple I's, our Eye into the outside world. You might equate them with computer screens." Legna paused.

Andrew asked, "How can you look at that crystal pyramid and see what we would normally see on a computer screen? I don't see any wires. Do you have access to satellites and WIFI up here?"

"No, it uses telepathy. You direct your gaze toward the Eye and project what you want to know. It returns images and text based on your telepathic request. Images appear in front of you with no need for a computer screen or even a keyboard. Now, I will leave you here to practice and look up whatever you want. I have programmed them to accept your brainwaves as authorized users. There will be some limitations on your information access. For instance, my crew has access to the schematics of the ship. If you want some of that information, you will have to come to me for access.

"Have fun with your research, enjoy the ship, and partake in a nice meal. Tomorrow morning Archangel Michael will join us in the Astral Room."

Chapter 21 – First Look:
Featuring Archangel Barachiel

The following morning, with their minds overloaded with the ship's marvels along with the anticipation of their journey to the new planet to witness the dawn of a new age, excitement charged the atmosphere aboard the ship.

After a quick breakfast, Legna escorted the excited group to the Astral Room. The twinkling sparkles of thousands of stars spilled out into the hallway.

As Legna announced that Archangel Michael was waiting inside, their elation escalated to an even higher level. Angie exclaimed what they have all surmised as they stepped through the myriad of stars, "Archangel Orion!"

Michael got right down to business to tamp down the excitement and keep to the task at hand. "Good morning, and please be seated. You are aware that the residents of Tenalp go through the Veil of Forgetfulness. Therefore, they do not remember that their life's purpose is to stay on a loving path as needed to help improve their karma. Your primary task will be to observe those veering off the path and report your findings to the archangels. Orion will be able to speed back and forth with updated information."

The serious tone in the room turned jovial when Orion greeted them with a "Good morning! I was in the area to check on the orbits of a comet and asteroid and decided to stop by for a quick visit. I must be on my way to spread love among the stars. Perhaps you will see me."

He was gone in a flash, a cascade of stars trailing behind him. They scampered over to an Astral Room porthole to catch a glance of Orion, who stopped in mid-air, turned around, and nodded toward them. It appeared as if he was standing on the dazzling blue ion trail of a comet. He took off again with his silhouette charging the distant galaxies with luminaries radiating far and wide before he was out of sight.

"Let's return to our seats," Michael continued. "When we meet on Mount Overlook, I will introduce you to Archangel Barachiel, who has dominion over lightning and storms. His current assignment is to introduce fire to the community."

"I have a concern. May I ask a question?" Mary politely asked.

"Yes, you may," replied Archangel Michael.

"Will they be able to see us or our craft?"

"No. A cloaking device shrouds the craft," Michael explained. "You will either transport, or you will travel by a smaller shuttlecraft with Legna. We will assemble at Mount Overlook, where the foliage will provide cover. Now, I must go." Without further ado, Archangel Michael was gone.

The startled group remained motionless stunned at Michael's quick departure. "We have so many more questions," stated Andrew.

"Come. Let's go to the Observation Deck," invited Legna. "All of your questions will be answered in due time."

The group turned gleeful at the thought of their upcoming adventure and quickly strapped themselves into their seats.

"We're finally on the way!" shouted Angie. The others expressed their excitement in heightened tones.

"I understand your eagerness. However, please do not speak out loud. My crew needs to focus on navigating," instructed Legna. "We can all read each other's minds, but my crew can tune out mental chatter much more easily."

"Sorry!" said Angie on behalf of them all.

They watched planets and stars whiz by. At times they thought they saw Orion or was it a shooting star? Before long, Legna ordered the craft to warp speed, and they lunged forward into the starlit abyss. The colors of elongated stars and colorful images zipped past. Anticipation ignited their minds with thoughts of what they would see and do once they reached there. They had seen a video, but now they were about to experience the real thing.

Will the land look like Earth? What about flowers, trees, birds and animals? What about the people? Angie thought.

The instant they dropped out of warp speed, their minds quieted. They craned their necks as they tried to decern every detail that came into view.

Angie politely asked, "Are we there yet?" She knew in their collective thoughts that they were all wondering the same thing.

Legna stood behind their chairs. "Yes, we are here, and you may get up now." They hastily unfastened their seatbelts and rushed toward the observation windows to observe a closer glimpse of the planet. Even though they were still up very high, they could see landmasses and bodies of water through wispy clouds.

"We must be going," announced Legna. We will now leave the Mother Ship and transport to the shuttlecraft. Please hold hands."

Once settled into the shuttle, Legna became a tour guide, saying, "Look toward the right, and you will see the planet that we call Tenalp. See that high peak? That is Mount Overlook."

Angie loved the video tour they watched with Mariel, but it was nothing compared to the real thing.

Legna snapped their attention back to the present with his announcement, "It is time to go down closer, but we are not going to transport. Instead, we will take this shuttlecraft, giving you a better opportunity to see large segments of the planet up close. This shuttle has a cloaking device so that we won't frighten anyone."

As they drew closer, they could see that the planet looked lush with greenery. The treetops created a dense canopy hiding the community below. It looked just like the planet earth.

Angie was eager to observe every detail and commented, "It is like a rain forest but missing the colorful parrots and monkeys."

Legna continued, "We will land in an unoccupied area below the canopy to observe the living conditions more closely."

Legna could sense their heightened exhilaration as a flood of comments invaded their minds. *Look at this! Look at that! Look over there! Did you see that?*

As they descended, Mary pointed out, "The inhabitants have crude wrappings around their thin bodies. It is hard to imagine how they can make their clothing without the use of needle and thread." The others agreed.

A cave came into view with an enormous entrance so large they could drive the shuttle right in if they wanted to, but it was dark inside. Legna made a suggestion. "No one is inside or near the cave. We will park the shuttle directing a spotlight inside. Then, we can take a brief look allowing you to observe their living quarters. To avoid being detected, we must act fast." In a flash, they were in, quickly looked around, and were out again.

"Did you see their leaf and straw beds on the floor? It must be so uncomfortable. It felt damp too. No wonder everyone is outside in the sunlight," remarked Mary.

This settlement is certainly primitive beyond anything we could have imagined. The people of Tenalp have no idea of the comforts they were missing. The others agreed with Angie's thoughts.

As they lifted off, they all looked back to see fields teeming with flowers and children chasing butterflies. Some rabbits scampered away from the activities. Birds darted between the tree branches. A ribbon of water was crowded with people. The pathways were no more than tamped down dirt. They witnessed a very crude living environment filled with people dealing with their living conditions.

They landed the craft back on Mount Overlook and found their favorite gazebo in the clearing with lightning bolts flashing in every direction. As they adjusted their eyes, they could see an Archangel donned in a lush green robe. Smaller lightning bolts accentuated his stormy grey aura. In subtle contrast, rose petals edged his hemline while the scent of roses filled the air. Rose petals decorated the gazebo floor. He held a single white rose in one hand and a lightning bolt in the other. *It looks like we are in a lightning storm in a rose garden without the rain*, thought Mary.

"Hello everyone, I am Archangel Barachiel. I am the Archangel of Blessings and Sweetness hence the rose petals, and I also have dominion over lightning and storms. Archangels are neither male nor female but can appear as either, although most stick to the same persona time after time. Today, I have chosen to appear as a male. Do not be surprised if I appear to you as a female tomorrow." He nodded to Archangel Michael, who had joined them, along with a nod toward Legna.

As much as Angie was looking forward to her archangel hug, she hesitated because of the lightning bolts darting in all directions. Barachiel shifted his gaze down toward the rose petals. The others followed his glance, and unscathed, they received their archangels hugs.

Barachiel got right to the point. "Look at the people below. I asked the guardian angels to show themselves to you. Each soul has at least one."

As they looked, they could see angels everywhere. Angie remarked, "What a lovely welcome sight! Do the people know their guardian angels are there with them? Do they talk to them?"

Barachiel explained, "Yes, they know, especially the children. Children on Earth had their invisible playmates, their angels. When they learned abstract thinking, most could no longer see or hear them. On this planet, there is no advanced education to dispel the notion of angels. A guardian angel may elect to be visible or to stay out of sight, allowing a soul to experience feelings like fear and compassion on its own.

As if Barachiel spoke directly to her, Mary asked, "Are there predatory animals, dangerous insects, and poisonous foods?"

Archangel Michael replied, "Yes, Mary, there are numerous dangers. Many souls chose to live short lives on this planet so they can return to the astral plane, review this life, and plan their next incarnation. Dangers are part of the cycle of life and are a teaching tool.

Archangel Barachiel continued. "The Archangels and I have decided that it is time to introduce fire to this primitive planet. The event will be a significant milestone that will dramatically change their lives. It will keep them warm, provide light, and help them see the threats that lurk in the shadows after dusk. Over time, they will experiment with cooking, and cooked fish will become a favorite. It will bring laughter and joy to their lives which is one of my goals."

Angie, Andrew, Mary, and Matthew listened with excited amazement. They were going to witness the advent of fire. Together, they silently shared their thoughts of the extraordinary life they had with all the conveniences, more than they could possibly imagine.

"That is the answer," exclaimed Andrew. "We believe we have all we could ever imagine, and yet we don't know what the future holds in store for us. These people can't imagine beyond what they already have. We need to help them with new advances, like fire."

Chapter 22 – The Miracle of Fire

Barachiel continued with his preparations to introduce fire, "Before you ask how, a plan has been under development for quite some time. The people must experience fire and learn about it. They will see the lightning bolt come from the sky and hit a dead tree. They will understand that water will put the fire out, and they will learn so much more through a very educational plan. Look to the east of the clearing, and you will see a dead tree about 5 to 6 feet tall. It is sufficiently decayed and is ready to be part of my plan. We shall begin. Enjoy the show."

The tree was a perfect candidate for the advent of fire. It still wore its crown of dead leaves, rustling in the wind. When the sky grew ominous, the frightened community ran for cover into the haven of their cave. They crowded on top of each other. In the total darkness, uncontrollable tremors reverberated among them. Their bodies jumped with every crack of thunder while the flashes of lightning threw menacing shadows on the walls. Young ones screamed and cried, unable to find solace in the quaking arms of their caregivers.

With one final crash, a bolt of lightning splintered the designated tree in two like a mighty ax swinging down from the heavens. The ground shook violently, scaring the cave dwellers toward the entrance, ready to flee. They peered outside and found the two halves of the tree trunk aglow. The leaves of the dried headdress were crackling and scorching the hewn logs.

Archangel Barachiel pursed his mighty lips and sent the storm hurtling out over the wind-whipped ocean. The thunderous booms subsided.

At first, only a couple of brave souls cautiously ventured into the clearing, staring at the flames in disbelief. Slowly, the curious dared to leave the shelter of their sanctuary trepidatiously. There was silence except for an occasional crackle. Mesmerized, they were fascinated as the dry leaves caught fire, curled, and turned to ash. Panic had melted into wonder as they threw on more dried leaves. The firelight's reflection danced in their eyes.

A gigantic male with muscles like an ox grabbed an unburned end of one of the logs and dragged it into the cave. Firelight illuminated the interior while playful shadows danced along the walls. Shadow puppets added to their newfound merriment.

Guardian angels warned their charges to stay clear, explaining that they could catch fire as quickly as the dried leaves. The older folk tried experimenting with cooking vessels. Boiling water piqued their curiosity. Fires died down, and more leaves and twigs revived the flames. Teaching moments abounded.

"This is wonderful and amazing," commented Andrew. "Thank you for the opportunity to witness this marvel along with the community's reactions.

Archangel Barachiel commented, "and so it has come to pass. Their lives will forever evolve as they experiment."

Archangel Orion spread a blanket of stars over the clearing to signal that it was time for the community to sleep. The young slept on their crude mattresses. They turned away from the light and felt the warmth of the fire on their backs. The adults continued experimenting with the fire while the children were fast asleep and out of harm's way.

Archangel Michael announced, "We accomplished good work this day. It is time for you to return with Legna to his craft to rest and be ready for the next phase in developing this planet. I bid you goodnight."

The foursome took the shuttle back, and in no time at all, they were standing In the Communication and Research Center on the mothercraft.

Legna stood before them and advised, "I have to attend to some business. Tomorrow morning, we will return to Tenalp."

"Legna?" inquired Angie. "I am so worried about those people. They don't understand fire and could burn themselves or start a forest fire. Shouldn't we continue to watch over them? I'll go back if you let me. I don't know what I can do, but I can try."

"Angie, your heart is so pure, and your concern for everyone is known by the legions of angels and Archangels. Don't worry. There are two Archangels you will meet tomorrow, Archangels Nathaniel and Ariana. They are there now, and all those people have at least one guardian angel watching over them. The intent of introducing them to fire was not to harm them or their lands but to help them. Archangel Nathaniel has dominion over fire. We couldn't ask for a better protector. Angie, thank you for your offer and your sincere caring, which I know is shared by all of you. It is a pleasure and privilege to be your friend. Now, I must return to the Observation Deck."

As he headed toward the door, Legna mentioned, "Now that you have toured the craft, you may venture anywhere you want. Laem can help you put a meal together. Enjoy and have a good night's rest."

They enjoyed some delicacies and, exhausted, returned to their sleeping quarters. Angie and Andrew sat on the edge of one bed while Matthew and Mary sat on the edge of the other. In unison, they fell backward. The mattresses seemed alive as they reached up and molded to their bodies. Quickly, Angie and Mary turned toward their guys so they could cuddle before the mattress filled the space between them.

"I love these mattresses. They are so comfortable. I want one at home," stated Angie. They all agreed. Angie added, "Let's do a quick meditation as we drift off to sleep. Three deep breaths and let your mind drift off to a happy place." They were all fast asleep in no time.

The sleeping quarter door opened, and they all sat straight up. Legna was back, letting them know morning had arrived. "We will return to Tenalp soon. Time to get ready. We will meet in the Communication and Research Center after you get some nourishment."

When they gathered, Legna was the first to speak. "I am anticipated some people may have been burned. They will need to find the Aloe Vera plant to use as a poultice. It will be interesting to see if they have figured out how to cook fish. They will need to find bamboo, and they will need to soak the bamboo first, so it doesn't catch fire. Their guardian angels will be able to help with these things by putting thoughts in their minds. Remember, life cannot be made too easy for them, but Angels can nudge them in the right direction. By now, they have probably realized that rainwater puts the outdoor fire out and will realize that water will put out any fires that get out of hand. Our mission is to observe and discuss how we can help without interfering. The Archangels will be there. Nathaniel, with his dominion over fire, will be able to make suggestions. Ariana is there working with the children, so we need to talk to her and find out her challenges. Let's go."

They held hands and arrived on Mount Overlook where they had been the day before. At first glance, everything looked fine. The logs were still burning in the clearing and tree in the cave. People were milling about and chattering. There was a sense of wonder and joy in the air.

The young children were gleefully playing. Some were climbing trees while others were hanging upside down from the tree limbs. More were chasing butterflies in a grassy field. Their young minds had enough of the fire for now.

Chapter 23 – Karma & The Wee Ones:
Featuring Archangels Nathaniel & Ariana

They were all anxious to make sure everyone was doing well with their introduction to fire, so they hurried and arrived on Tenalp before their meeting time with the Archangels.

Legna made a suggestion. "It looks like everything is fine but let's read their minds and see if they have any concerns. Angie, take the North; Andrew, the South; Mary, the East; and, Matthew, the West. I'll check in with Nathanial and Ariana. It won't take us long and if someone moves into your area, read their mind. I would rather have their mind read twice than not at all. Look for concerns, questions, and worries. It will be interesting to discover their reactions. Remember to stay out of sight. We will meet back here."

When everyone returned, Legna asked, "Did any of you find any concerns to report?"

They all responded in unison with, "No."

Mary said, "It was nice to read their thoughts and find out how much they love the warmth of the fire. They have slept in the cold for a very long time."

"I noticed that too," said Angie. "Some have been experimenting with cooking fish by weaving it on a stick."

"That is good news. The angels are doing a wonderful job. It is time for us to meet with Archangel Michael," declared Legna.

Archangel Michael appeared before them in his majestic blue robes and holding his mighty sword. A backdrop of twinkling stars signaled that Orion had also joined them.

"Good morning!" announced Michael with Orion echoing, "Good morning!"

"The next archangels you will meet are Archangel Nathaniel and his twin flame Archangel Ariana who work as a team. Nathaniel helps people work out their karma. On Tenalp, when people go through the Veil of Forgetfulness and have free will, they may need help staying on the loving path. We cannot interfere, but we can nudge them along.

Instantly, flames seemed to intermingle with the starlight from Orion. A tall, muscular archangel with long brown hair appeared before them. Nathaniel's robe was bright red with streaks of orange, resembling the flames of an intense fire. It was mesmerizing, like watching a fireplace. Gentle breezes tugged at his gown, making the fire seem to shoot higher. His aura appeared to be on fire, with red flames blazing around his head. In one hand, he held a jagged thunderbolt. In the other, a red candle.

Nathaniel nodded toward Michael and Orion and then stepped forward and bowed to the foursome with his wings spread, inviting them for archangel hugs. Even though he appeared to be on fire, his hug was cool and gentle. Any heat was from the sincerity of his warm embrace.

"Nice to meet all of you. I am Archangel Nathaniel. I have dominion over the energy of fire, and I also bring balance, harmony, and trust, especially during significant life changes. The candle I hold clears all that doesn't serve the highest good. Light a red candle and watch the negativity burn and float away.

"Before I go on, I would like to introduce you to Archangel Ariana. She helps the children and helps their souls' transition to a higher enlightenment. She will explain more later."

Angie couldn't help but stare at this amazing Archangel that reminded her of Cleopatra, very stoic and regal. Her green eyes sparkled like emeralds. She wore a calming powdery blue tunic and pants accented with silver. A silver headband made of crystals encircled her jet-black hair, highlighting her aura. In one hand, she held a crystal wand. Her other hand, although empty, had a healing gentleness. Angie could imagine her putting her hand on the shoulders of the wee ones to calm them. She stood tall and serious but exuded a gentleness that they sensed as she offered them her archangel hugs.

Nathaniel explained, "The primary purpose for the souls living on Tenalp is to repair their damaged karma. They have taken all the required steps to earn the privilege of starting on this next leg of their journey. The problem is that they will not remember why they are here and what they must do. That is where we come in. The angels, Archangels, and all of you must encourage them to stay on a loving path. It might sound simple, but our job is behind the scenes without accelerating or hindering their progress. With the help of the Guardian Angels, we can nudge them in the right direction. Actions are like a boomerang. That which you send forth returns to you either to enrich or to damage your karma.

Archangel Michael requested, "Nathaniel, please explain the difference between an advanced and primitive karmic repair."

"Sure, and that is a good point. Sometimes a soul will select a type of life to balance a prior negative act. For instance, if a soul was greedy in a previous life, it may choose to live a life of poverty. If a soul was cruel to others, it might elect to be the subject of negative behavior. That is advanced karma. However, on this primitive planet, those choices are not yet available. They have one mission and one mission only, and that is to stay on the loving path and to fill their souls with unbounded love."

"That makes sense," added Mary. "If everyone stays on a loving path, there won't be any negative options."

"Yes, Mary. That is exactly right. All we have to do to achieve balance and harmony is to keep everyone on that path," Orion replied.

"I also have dominion over fire energy," stated Nathaniel. "After Archangel Barachiel's introduction to fire, this is a perfect time to assist with the major lifestyle change on Tenalp along with my twin flame, Ariana."

Using this as an introduction, Nathanial asked, "Ariana, will you explain your tasks?"

Ariana clarified, "My expertise is with the children. Please pay close attention to them. Watch for signs on their faces and in their body language. They will face adversity in all shapes and sizes and will need our help deciphering their emotions. I will help them from behind the scenes and will work closely with their Guardian Angels."

"Now, as we leave to tend to our tasks among the community, I must emphasize," Nathaniel continued, "love must be the theme for all. Everyone must experience unrequited love."

Michael spoke. "Thank you, Nathanial, Ariana, and Orion. It is time for you to move forward with your mission. I wish you success."

"Until we meet again, we bless you with an outpouring of love," offered Ariana. With that, they were gone.

Michael nodded goodbye as he left, and the gazebo vanished from view.

"Let's get back to the spacecraft. You will have some free time. Please get a good night's rest as we have another full day planned for tomorrow," instructed Legna. They held hands and were back on board. Before they could ask any questions, Legna left them and retreated to his office.

Chapter 24 – Trip to Somewhere

They had a relaxing night with nothing in particular to do, so they visited the Communication and Research Center and checked out pictures and articles about Earth II. When their nostalgia got the best of them, they virtually spoke to Wendy and William and a few of the kids. All was well, and they promised to check in again soon.

Before they went to bed, Archangel Michael summoned them to the Astral Room, where Legna was also waiting. Michael addressed them. "Legna has invited you to visit a unique and very advanced planet, Nerrab. You will find this trip very interesting and informative. We will continue with our work on Tenalp when you return. I bid you farewell."

Despite Michael's departure, a floodgate of questions gushed forth like an unbridled stream. "When will we go?" "Will we transport there?" "How long will they stay?" "What do the people look like?" "Who are they?" "Is the planet as beautiful as Earth II?" "Will they treat us to a meal like Zcar and Hcar did?"

Legna anticipated the questions, and when it grew quiet, he realized that everyone was looking to him for answers. "We will travel aboard this craft. Our schedule will be determined after I attend to some business. You will meet my family and enjoy a meal with them. My planet is very different, and I'm sure you will find it fascinating. Enough questions. No more clues for now. We will arrive by daybreak. Get a good night's rest, and I'll let you know when we arrive."

Wind chimes woke them, so they quickly got ready, dressing a little nicer than usual, knowing that something special was in the air. Legna's voice announced, "We have arrived, and you will want to witness the descent to my planet."

Laem met them along the way and handed them breakfast sandwiches and juice as they rushed to the observation platform. They were disappointed when a totally barren planet came into view. There were no trees or vegetation. It looked like the moon's surface, craters and all.

Legna could sense their disappointment and warned, "Be still and watch. I promise you. A surprise awaits."

The spacecraft came to a halt, and engines were turned off. Unfamiliar silence replaced the hum they had grown accustomed to. After a brief moment, the craft started to move downward. As they descended, other spacecraft came into view, parked beneath the surface. When they arrived at the bottom, they were towed to a parking bay.

"The spacecraft will be serviced while we are here," advised Legna. "This is my home planet. I welcome you on behalf of my people."

Angie's mind was on overload. "Wow, Legna. I always wanted to visit your planet and meet your family. How many children do you have? How do you get your water and light down here? What about your food?"

"You have so many questions, and we will answer them soon. Follow me as we disembark the ship. Be sure to look up. You will see that the pad we landed on has returned to the surface. To all those that pass by, they will think this is an uninhabited planet and not worth their time."

With their eyes looking skyward, they followed Legna. They couldn't help but notice that the pad's underside, a perfect circle, was smooth but was surrounded by gems showering light on the areas below.

Andrew was curious. "There are no visible wires or movable parts. How does the pad move?"

Legna explained, "You are familiar with the use of crystals on Earth II. Crystals provide our power here, as well. They are providing light, energy, and a means of transport. You will see more of their uses during our tours."

The foursome nodded as Legna continued. "Before you is the start of our subterranean farmland. We grow our food hydroponically under crystal light, and large fans circulate the air for pollination purposes. Some pollination is done by hand since we don't have bees on our planet. There are no pests, diseases, or weeds."

They sat in silence, watching enormous farmlands stretch as far as their eyes could see. Greenery, mixed with the bright colors of fruits and vegetables, continued for miles in all directions. The crystal planting beds sparkled and twinkled, continually capturing their interest.

"Let's pause here," suggested Legna.

Angie was mesmerized by the dazzling beauty of the quartz planting beds and the highly polished floors. The quartz reflected light everywhere.

"Where are the farmers and workers?" asked Andrew.

Legna explained, "When a family removes a plant for consumption, they are required to replace it with a new plant. They must also start new seedlings for the future. The cycle of our food chain moves smoothly and divides the tasks among everyone."

"Legna, I don't see any flowers for cutting and displaying in vases," inquired Mary.

"You will not find any. We do not waste our space growing flowers to destroy them for enjoyment. The beautiful colors of the crystals beautify our colony. Beyond the farmlands, you will see a forest of fruit and nut trees."

"Do the leaves change colors and drop off? What kind of trees do you grow?" asked Angie.

"My wife will take you to visit the farmlands while she gathers produce for our dinner meal. She will give you a guided tour and answer your questions. There is so much to see. Meanwhile, please take a seat on the transporter. It is a long journey to our dwellings."

The transporter, as Legna referred to it, was quite comfortable and reminded the travelers of a moving walkway in an airport but complete with relaxing seats. During their ride, they were mesmerized watching the farmlands pass by. They tried to recognize the different crops. Corn, tomatoes, and eggplant had their telltale signatures, but there was so much more.

Chapter 25 – The Crystal Residence

Lost in their identification quest, they found themselves at the end of the line. An exquisite colossal archway greeted the guests, radiating a blinding light, making them wonder what lay beyond.

Legna stood at the front and explained, "Here is the entrance to our subterranean living communities. The first room is our communal area, known as the diamond room. It is also the source of our water and much of our energy. Follow me but first put on these eye shield visors."

Silence filled the room except for an occasional gasp as they beheld the magnificent sights, pleasant sounds and witnessed the enormity that lay before them.

"I want to see everything up close," stated Angie as she tilted her visor up. An excruciating squeal of agony pierced the calm. "I'm blinded!" she cried as she flipped the visor back down.

"Angie, be warned. The intense glare of the crystals will damage your eyes. Do not take off your visor until I tell you," warned Legna. They all took heed, and he continued.

"As your eyes adjust, you will see the vastness of our community area. I would estimate the non-water sections to be about four football fields containing every size and shape of diamonds. Although the majority are clear, you will find a variety of colors that accentuate while calming the blinding nature of the bright diamonds."

"Look," Mary suggested as she pointed toward the waterfall. "The blue diamonds give the water a perfect tropical color."

Legna took a moment to explain further. "The color blue has positive effects on the mind and the body. Its presence can cause the body to produce calming chemicals, slowing the metabolism, resulting in tranquility and providing balance."

They gazed at the beauty before them. At one end, a waterfall skipped merrily toward the massive lake. Ripples found their way across the calm waters offering a little splash when they reached the diamond banks. The ceiling of yellow and blue diamonds resembled sunlight streaming across a blue sky. There were no other materials anywhere. Some surfaces were highly polished, giving the appearance of glass, while the irregular surfaces radiated diamond rainbows and sunbeams in all directions.

"Legna, why don't you have to wear an eye visor?" asked Angie while she scrutinized every nook and cranny of this magnificent area.

"Our eyes have a protective membrane that serves as a shield, whether we are here among the crystals or traversing the universe encountering the brilliance of the suns."

Satisfied with Legna's response, Angie asked, "Are the seats comfortable without cushions?"

"Although we are slim by nature, our skin is thick and buoyant. We find the seats comfortable for our body types. Find your own comfort level. You may sit or stand. Enjoy the scene for a moment while I announce our arrival."

The foursome talked among themselves, raving about the beauty before them and marveling at the use of crystals, far beyond anything they had experienced on Earth II.

"My wife is ready to welcome you," Legna announced upon his return. "Please follow me. You may remove your visor when we pass through the next entryway. Keep them with you for the future."

As they stepped through an archway, half spheres of sparkling green emeralds lined the walls, providing sufficient light to illuminate their way. The highly polished floors were smooth but not slippery. The corridor disappeared far into the distance with occasional bright patches of light, like sunbeams, reflecting outward along the route.

They hadn't traveled very far when Legna turned into a sunny archway and announced, "We are here. Rednow, I would like you to meet Angie, Andrew, Mary, and Matthew."

They exchanged greetings while their eyes greedily feasted on more gems. The living quarters were Saffire blue. The theme of highly polished flat floors with the walls adorned with rounded crystal half-spheres continued throughout. Only the ceilings maintained their multifaceted shapes.

"Everything is so beautiful. How did you ever mine all these gems? Did you have to dig deep into the planet? And how did you smooth them? And who might that be, hiding behind you and clinging to your leg?" Angie asked as she stared around the room again and again.

"This is our female offspring, Ria. She is about three of your earth years. She is shy because she hasn't seen beings that look different from us," explained Rednow. "In time, she will become comfortable and emerge from her safety zone behind me.

Legna picked up the conversation, "Crystals are a commodity throughout the universe. Many civilizations associate them with monetary wealth, while others appreciate their energy-producing properties."

"I understand," confirmed Andrew. "On Earth I, they had monetary value. Crystals provide the source for lighting and transportation on Earth II."

"But how did you mine such beautiful crystals, and how long did it take?" asked Andrew in his never-ending quest for knowledge.

Legna gladly provided a brief summarization of the history of his planet. "Crystals are located right beneath the surface, and there was and is no seismic activity to damage or dirty the gems. Our ancestors spent eons cutting and polishing them. Our flooring needed to be smooth yet not slippery. Our walls needed to be free from jagged edges while providing sufficient light. Thus, the hemisphere effect. We selected the colors for maximum effectiveness, similar to our waterfalls. We use a calming blue color for living quarters."

"Why aren't all planets created like this one?" asked Andrew.

"Do you use any crystals as currency?" asked Angie.

"These are very valid questions," continued Legna. "From the beginning of time, all civilizations were given planets with specific attributes to adapt and conquer. The goal was to have multitudes of successful but diverse civilizations throughout the galaxies. Many have succeeded while others have failed as you saw with Earth I."

"Oh, yes. We certainly experienced that," stated Angie. "The occupants of Earth II were introduced to crystals along with many other improvements for the betterment of everyone."

Legna acknowledged Angie's comment with a nod and said, "My people were selected to be the custodians of this planet without greed. There is no need for a monetary system. Everyone works together for the benefit of all."

Mary, concerned for the future of this beautiful planet, asked, "Aren't you afraid that someone will find you and try and take your gems?"

"It is a concern that if someone were to discover us and mine our crystals, our colony would fail based on another's desire for wealth and power. That is why we appear to be a barren planet. We don't invite visitors. However, since you have demonstrated that you have our best interest at heart, you have been granted a special honor by Archangel Michael, and my people have consented to your visit. You may not discuss our adventure with others outside the astral plane."

Legna guided them forward with a gesture. "Come! Let me show you more. Please enter."

Rednow shadowed them, with Ria in tow.

He ushered them through another archway. "This is my family's Communication and Research Center."

Angie observed the same pyramid crystals that were in the Communication and Research Center aboard the spacecraft, the *Eyes*.

"Let us continue."

Chapter 26 – Home and Garden

He led them through another archway where they saw a couple of younger aliens sitting in front of activated Eyes. "These are our two male offspring. They are Nos and Yob."

"They look just like you, Legna," Mary deduced. "Yet, I can tell them apart by their thoughts."

Nos and Yob glanced over their shoulders with a nod and went quickly back to their Eyes.

"What information can they access?" asked Andrew.

"We have access to all information throughout the galaxies. Our civilization must be universally aware. For our offspring, we limit the inquisition scope as a teaching and learning tool. The more they learn, the more information they may retrieve. We all have an infinite thirst for knowledge. However, our learning capabilities are based on a growth algorithm. The more math and science you learn, the more receptive you are to additional education."

"I certainly have a thirst for knowledge!" interjected Angie, which made them all laugh in agreement.

"Legna, when you travel to the other planets, how often can you come back to be with your family?" asked Mary.

Before Legna could respond, Angie asked, "Do you visit as a hologram?"

"I shall answer Mary first. Many of us travel to other planets to offer help, seen or unseen. We are universally aware and can assist when the Archangels need a physical presence. We have been granted the ability of astral projection because of our devoted universal assistance. We transport when we think of our destination.

"Angie, there are times we use a type of hologram called Isogram or an Isomorphic projection. A hologram is merely an interactive picture, but an Isogram is a three-dimensional shape that contains the same crystalline form as the emitter. It can walk, talk, consume, and interact like an actual being."

"Why would you use an isogram when you can astral project?" asked Angie.

"A good example would be multi-tasking. We can be in two places simultaneously, and although we can act separately from our Isogram, two locations can observe us. It is beneficial with meeting scheduling.

"Is this gelatinous material the same substance used in the spacecraft?"

"Good observation and question, Angie. Yes, it allows our ships to morph into different shapes, enhancing our maneuverability. Most planets have not discovered this chemical composition."

Legna led them through another archway. "This is our resting room. It was similar to a bedroom you might find on Earth II but without the frills, and it accommodates us all in one area."

"Crystal platforms without blankets or mattresses?" observed Angie.

"Our bodies like hard surfaces and our environmental controls negate the need for blankets," countered Legna.

"There are no decorations. No wall paintings. It is so bare," suggested Mary, who loves to decorate.

Legna was quick to point out, "This is a room where we sleep. With eyes closed, it is pointless to clutter with trinkets or decorations. In our living areas, our crystals provide the beauty our beings desire."

As they moved on, Legna explained. "This is our main gathering area, combined with our nutrition area. Please have a seat at the table. Rednow has prepared a meal for you to enjoy. I'll tell our offspring to join you, but I will eat later. First, I have some business to attend to."

They could hear Legna say, "Disconnect. Come join our guests for nourishment."

"Salad. We love salads," commented Mary.

Rednow explained, "We do not cook our food. We eat vegetables, fruit, nuts, and seeds—garden to the table. I have prepared a salad containing many different items. Please enjoy."

"Do you have any salad dressing?" asked Matthew.

"No. We do not disguise our food. I hope you will find favor with it," replied Rednow.

Angie, who had already taken a bite, quickly retorted, "I'm sure we will. Matthew, I believe you will find that the juiciness of some foods complements the crispiness of the other ingredients. It is very delicious. Nothing else is needed."

No one spoke a word while they ate. When the last of the diners set their forks down, Angie reverted to her previous comment, "See, Matthew. You don't need anything else when you have the right pairings. Right?"

"Absolutely. I enjoyed every morsel. Thank you, Rednow," replied Matthew as the others joined in with their compliments and thanks.

The young ones asked if they could leave the table. Rednow had different ideas. "Yes, you may. However, I would like you to show our guests what you are studying while I clean up. Then we will take them for a tour of the gardens. We can pick ingredients for our next meal, and you can show them how to replant and start new seedlings."

Without a complaint, they hurried to their computers, with their guests, except Mary, who stayed behind and asked, "May I help you, Rednow?"

"Oh no, my dear. You will learn much more from our sons, and there isn't much to clean up. Please go ahead."

Mary joined the others and listened while the *Eye* danced from topic to topic with explanations raining forth. They thoroughly impressed their guests.

Rednow called out, "Time to go to the gardens."

They quickly joined Rednow. Ria's comfort level was evident. She moved from behind Rednow to next to her while still holding her mother's hand. "Guests, please remember to put your visors on when we enter the community room."

As Legna referred to them, the' male offspring' rushed on as if anticipating a grand adventure. They breezed through the communal area, oblivious to other occupants.

Angie was the first one to remove her visor. "These gardens are so beautiful." The youngsters, including Ria, rushed up and down the aisles, pointing out ripened vegetables. Rednow hurried behind them, gathering the prized selections.

Rednow commented, "It is good for the children to take a pause from the 'Eyes' and run the farmlands. They will let me know if I have missed a delicious ingredient. Please feel free to roam. Let me know if you have any questions."

Angie and Mary walked together, talking about ingredients and recipes, recognizing lots of vegetables, and wondering about the unfamiliar produce's name and taste.

As they walked through the rows of crystal growing beds, Andrew and Matthew discussed the structures and hydroponics.

Several football fields far in the distance revealed an orchard full of towering, majestic trees with bowed branches laden with their fruit offerings. Rednow had caught up to them, so Angie asked, "What kind of trees are they? What happens when they drop their leaves?"

"All those trees you see are fruit and nut trees. Our crystals generate a constant temperature ideal for growing all our produce. Our trees are genetically modified to adapt. The leaves do not change color and drop off. When an occasional leaf does fall, fans blowing a gentle breeze at the base push the leaves toward our compost heap."

Thinking of the change of seasons or lack thereof, Angie commented, "Earth II is like that. I didn't know if I would like it at first, but I do. I suppose I miss the budding of trees signaling the start of Spring, and the reds, oranges, and yellow autumn leaves, like big puffy bonnets, that were always a sight to behold. I do not miss the barren trees reaching up to the heavens signifying the winter death of the growing season."

"Oh, but how we love to be able to grab a piece of fruit at any time of the year," announced Matthew as he grabbed an apple and took a big bite.

"A compost heap! The circle of plant life!" marveled Angie.

"Yes, indeed," agreed Rednow. "All food scraps are turned into compost and fuel for our entire hydroponic system."

"Nos. Yob," Rednow called out. "Please deposit our prior meal's surplus in the compost heap, and don't forget to give the armature a spin to embed our scraps within the others.

The group watched as the children ran up, grabbed the waste, and ran back with Ria scrambling behind. The boys even helped Ria turn the handle a full rotation.

Chapter 27 – Getting to Know Them

"Your children are so obedient and helpful," observed Angie.

"That is our lifestyle," explained Rednow. Everyone understands that we work together for the sake of the community. There is never a complaint or argument. We do not raise our voices except in song."

"Has it always been this way?" inquired Angie.

"Absolutely. It has been our way since the very beginning of time," explained Rednow. "Without a monetary system, there is no need for competition."

"We are grateful that they envisioned this planet and chose us to be the custodians. Legna and the others have visited so many planets and have learned the best ways to live, eat, and survive. Our "Eyes" connect us to the outside worlds for endless knowledge while we are safe and sound in our self-sustaining, loving world."

"You've thought of everything down here," remarked Angie. "But don't you miss not visiting with other people?"

"No," Rednow responded. When you lived on Earth, you did not know about other species and colonies. You had no way of knowing what you were missing. We are fortunate to have 'Eyes' to visit the vast universe. We are very content amongst ourselves."

"Nos! Yob! We have removed many plants. Please go to the nursery to gather the replacements and start some new seedlings. Take our guests with you and show them. Ria and I will stay here to help prepare the soil for replanting."

The foursome received quite an education as they watched the young ones select and transfer plants to a quartz planting wagon for transport. They sowed some seeds to encourage new seedling growth. Angie noticed the access to the compost heap. She saw a much smaller waterfall and pond in the nursery providing the water they needed to moisten the soil and for the hydroponic system.

The offspring planted the new plantings in all the vacant spaces.

"Nos, Yob, and Ria, you have done an excellent job. It is time to return home," announced Rednow, watching them run back to her side. "We have had enough exercise and fun for now."

Suddenly, Angie felt a small hand find its way into her grasp. Ria was holding both her Mom's hand and Angie's hand. She shared a smile with Rednow, acknowledging Ria's acceptance.

With visors back on, they passed through the community area. Rednow took them over to the lake, where crystal pitchers were available. They helped themselves to one, filled it with water, and continued on their way.

Before the young ones could retreat to their computers, Rednow offered everyone a glass of water.

"Wow, this tastes delicious. It is cold without ice cubes. So refreshing and satisfying," exclaimed Matthew.

"Yes, our water is refreshing. Please leave your goblets at your places at the table," instructed Rednow.

The youngsters dragged Andrew and Matthew back to their communication stations while Angie and Mary accompanied Rednow and Ria into the kitchen.

Angie picked up an onion, rolled it in her hands, and put it to her nose. "The fresh smell and texture are amazing."

Rednow instructed them with lots of slicing and dicing and even mashing of the juicy tomatoes with basil to accentuate the fresh crispy ingredients. They also prepared a fruit salad complete with some nuts and seeds they picked from the orchards.

"Do you drink anything besides water? Do you squeeze juice from the fruits?" asked Angie. "And do you get enough protein from these ingredients? Do you take vitamins?"

Rednow smiled as she replied. "We only drink water. There is a high water content in the fruits and vegetables we consume to hydrate us adequately and to eliminate the need for vitamins. The varieties of nuts and beans in our diet fulfill our nutritional requirements for protein. It is a very healthy diet, and we do not have any illnesses.

"How do you clean your wastewater from showers?"

"We don't use water for cleaning. The intensity of the crystals creates a cleaning ionization for our homes, bodies, and food. Our bodies take in only the amount of hydration we require with minimal waste. The majority of planets do not know about the efficient use of crystals."

"Our water supply on Earth II contains all the nutrients we need to sustain life. We eat food for enjoyment and not for necessity," explained Angie.

"I was aware of that and was happy to learn that you do eat for enjoyment so that we could share our bounty with you," replied Rednow.

Legna returned and helped himself to a small bowl of lunch while his sons rushed to greet him. They cried excitedly, "Father! Father! What news have you brought us?"

"Good afternoon. Did you enjoy your lunch and afternoon outing in the gardens?"

"Yes!" the boys exclaimed. "We helped find the best ingredients for Mother and then showed our guests how we replant and start new seedlings. It was an enjoyable afternoon. Can our guests stay for dinner and maybe into tomorrow too?"

"The news I bring everyone is that our ship has completed its required maintenance service and is ready to depart."

"No! No!" protested the boys. "Can't they at least stay for dinner? Guests from other planets never visit us. We want them to stay."

Legna made a pronouncement for all to hear. "Archangel Michael has summoned us. We must go. However, we will not leave until after dinner. I suggest you make the best use of your time together."

Without further protest, Nos and Yob headed toward the communications center asking their guests to join them. "Please show us your home on Earth II. You know so much about us. Help us learn about you. OK, Father?"

"Sure. I will join you. Rednow will let us know when it is time for dinner."

The children tapped the bars. The gelatinous material rose to meet the upper bar creating a viewing screen.

Andrew responded with a "Wow."

Legna used his mind to telepathically locate pictures of Earth II. The guests grew homesick as they watched their favorite places appear before their eyes. Angie pointed out the town square, and Andrew pointed out the airport where Legna parks his ship.

Angie commented, "as much as I hate to leave you, I must admit that I am anxious to return home and see our family, if only for a short time."

"So many different life forms here!" the youngsters pointed out.

"We have leprechauns, fairies, and so many more. They used to hide on Earth I, but now they live among us, and we love them all," explained Angie.

"Do you use telepathy, or do you speak in different languages? How can you understand each other?" asked Yob.

Andrew addressed the question. "It is a combination. We all use telepathy along with our verbal skills. If we can't understand their verbal conversation, we read each others' minds. It is quite effective."

"Dinner is ready," called out Rednow.

Legna tapped the workstation, and the gelatinous mass dropped down and took on the shape of the elongated tube. They hurried to take their places at the table.

"This is delicious," announced Matthew as he sampled from the two serving bowls before them.

Rednow explained the ingredients. "You have spaghetti squash flavored with mashed tomatoes and sprinkled with fresh basil and oregano."

"I selected the squash," proudly announced Nos.

"I helped plant the new squash," rivaled Ria, who now seemed to be very comfortable with all her new guests even when her mother was out of sight.

When everyone finished, Legna made the announcement, "It is time to say our goodbyes."

The guests thanked Rednow individually and hugged the children. "We will come back someday and visit again," promised Angie.

"Yes! Please do! You are always welcome here, right, Father?" Much to everyone's surprise, it was Ria issuing the invite to return.

They left the living quarters and traveled down the green corridor. Legna reminded them to put on their visors and slowly escorted them through the community center so they could have a last look around.

As they boarded the conveyance and took their seats, Angie extended appreciation on behalf of the group, "We thank you, Legna, for everything. Your planet is beautiful and fascinating. Your family is wonderful. We have so many memories to cherish." The others signaled their agreement audibly and by nodding their heads.

"We are here. Watch your step," cautioned Legna as the spacecraft came into view.

As they boarded the craft, Legna announced, "We will reach our destination in the morning. Have a pleasant night's sleep."

Angie and Andrew enjoyed snuggling in each other's arms. As they were falling off to sleep, Angie whispered, "I loved our visit, and I love you. Goodnight."

Andrew kissed her forehead as he quietly stated, "I love you too. It was fun. Goodnight, my love."

Part III
Lessons Learned

Chapter 28 – What Evil Lurks

Wind chimes announced the new day. Wonderful new memories raced through the scrapbooks of their minds as they got ready to meet Laem in the Nutrition Area.

Legna joined them, "I trust you all had an enjoyable visit to my homeworld."

"Yes, we did. Thank you. We love your planet and your family and look forward to keeping in touch with them," responded Angie dreamily as the others nodded their agreement.

"I'm sure they would love to hear from you. Remember, please do not invite my family to visit Earth II."

"We understand," replied Angie. "Next time we are home, we will take them on a virtual tour of our community."

"Thank you. That would be nice," Legna commented. "Since I was away from my workstation for a couple of days, I am burdened with tasks that can't wait. I will be busy this morning, so enjoy some free time."

Michael challenged Andrew, "how would you like to try a 3-dimensional chess game I found on the Eye?"

"Sure, I'll give it a try," agreed Andrew.

"I would like to work with Laem in the kitchen," advised Mary. "What about you, Angie?"

"I think I'll go to the observation deck and look around. I'll catch up with you guys later."

Angie had other things on her mind. She thought, *I really want to talk to Legna. This could be the perfect opportunity to get him alone.*

Angie said, "Legna. I'm so glad to see you up here. Do you have a minute where we can talk in private?"

"Sure. Come to my office."

Legna directed her toward a wall, and as he approached, the wall slid open, revealing a room. "Come in."

"I didn't know this was here. Thank you for meeting with me."

"No problem. What's on your mind?"

Angie hesitated, wondering where to begin. "I am concerned about the negative souls that will incarnate soon."

"Yes. I remember your outburst."

"Please don't remind me, but I'm concerned that the very negative souls aren't ready. I love the people on Tenalp. They have worked so hard and are so loving and caring. If any of the souls who haven't restored unconditional love in their hearts and incarnate too soon, it could be devastating."

"Have you mentioned this to Archangel Michael or any of the Archangels? I recall that many of them said you could reach out to them for guidance. Maybe this would be a good time."

"No, I haven't reached out to anyone yet. The Archangels think I am worrying too much. The souls have to be approved on the astral plane first, so they believe my apprehension is premature."

"Then, I ask you. Why do you question the readiness of any souls? Shouldn't you leave that up to those in power? Shouldn't you trust their judgment?"

"Yes. You are correct. I sincerely want every soul to have a chance to restore its karma. On the other hand, I have this unshakable feeling that something will go wrong. I feel ill every time I think about it."

"Okay. Let's see. You seem to be worrying about the future. Why don't you visit the astral plane and meet with those in charge of the non-loving souls? Find out firsthand how they are progressing and their timeline. Perhaps you will get the opportunity to express your concerns and get some valid responses. That is what I would suggest."

"That is a great idea. Why didn't I think of that? Can you please keep this conversation between us?"

"What you ask might not be possible. Your guardian angels are watching over you even as we speak. They report to the Archangels. Perhaps you should ask your guardian angels to guide you in the right direction. That would be reasonable."

"Once again, you are right. I don't want to take up any more of your time, and I thank you. You are a great friend, mentor, and teacher. I am blessed to have you in my life. Thank you, Legna. I'll be off to help Laem and Mary in the kitchen. Now how do I get out of here."

"Just walk up to the wall. "It automatically opens when you are on this side. On the other side, it will only open for me. I'm glad you think I helped with your dilemma. I wish you well, and I'm always available if you want to talk."

Angie met with Mary and Laem, who were with Tae collecting ingredients from the Hydroponic Growing Center. Angie, feeling much better, joined right in.

Legna knew his conversation with Angie was not private. No one was in the room, but he knew that the angels and Archangels were always aware. It wasn't long before he was summoned.

"Legna. Please meet me in the Astral Room," directed Archangel Michael. "Please come alone."

In a matter of minutes, they met, and Legna commented, "After my talk with Angie, I was not surprised to hear from you, Michael. I hope my suggestion was acceptable."

"Yes. I agree. It is time for Angie, Andrew, Mary, and Matthew to visit the Astral Plane, and this time to focus on the resting area and the non-loving souls. Since we don't have anything scheduled for this afternoon, I'll take them over. They can stay in the Meet-and-Greet area tonight and return here tomorrow. That will give you plenty of time to take care of your pressing matters. The next day, I will introduce them to Archangel Phanuel, the archangel who specializes in removing evil. That will be a perfect conclusion to this educational inquiry."

"I'll have them meet you here in an hour, Michael if that is acceptable to you.

"Until then." They nodded toward each other, and Archangel Michael was gone.

Legna stopped by the Multipurpose Room and asked Andrew and Matthew to join the others in the Nutrition Area.

When they were all together, Legna explained, "I have just met with Archangel Michael."

"Oh, no. We missed him," exclaimed Angie.

"He will be back in an hour to meet with you and to take you to the Astral Plane."

Seeing the look of concern on Angie's face, Legna continued. "He mentioned that you have not been back to the Meet-and-Greet area for quite some time, and aware of my work backlog, he has invited you to go to the Astral Plane this afternoon and then stay overnight."

Matthew was the first to proclaim his jubilant "Yay! Count me in."

"The Unicorns! I can't wait to see them," declared Mary with an air of whimsy in her voice.

Legna continued, "Yes, you will have time for all that, and Archangel Michael is making the arrangements. Angie, do not look worried. Michael liked my suggestion without expressing any hesitation."

"Oh, good," Angie exclaimed with a sigh of relief.

"What suggestion?" asked Andrew.

"You will soon find out. Now finish your meals, freshen up and assemble in the Astral Room. I will see you when you get back tomorrow."

Andrew and Matthew ran back to the Multipurpose Room to close out the game they were playing and rushed back to the Nutrition Area to eat and get ready for their trip.

Archangel Michael was waiting for them in the Astral Room. He swooped them up in his massive wings, and they found themselves in the lobby of the resting area.

"Archangel Jeremiel, my Golden Star Angel!" Angie exclaimed as she rushed to greet him with the others in close pursuit.

Jeremiel stood tall before them in his dark purple robe with golden lights sparkling around his halo, reflecting light in all directions like shooting stars.

Archangel Michael announced, "Archangel Jeremiel, the Archangel of Hope, will give you a tour, help you check in on the severely damaged souls, and make arrangements for you to speak to their counselors. Afterward, he will escort you back to the Meet-and-Greet area. I won't return for you until late tomorrow. May you have beneficial meetings and an enjoyable evening." And then he was gone.

Angie couldn't help but wonder what he thought about her talk with Legna, but it didn't matter. This visit will alleviate her concerns. Or so she hoped.

Jeremiel asked the group to follow him down a long corridor. They approached one room where angel counselors were talking with some souls. Some exchanges were calm, while others were engaged in an active dialogue. He explained, "The first group of non-loving souls have restored love in their hearts and are currently living on Tenalp. I understand they are doing quite well."

"Yes, they are," replied Angie. "Archangel Barachiel introduced them to fire, and we were there to witness that major milestone."

Jeremiel continued. "The next groups are currently working with counselors in the School of Wisdom. We will meet some of them tomorrow. They are on track to join the others on Tenalp, whether by birth or walk-in.

"Walk-in? I thought walk-in meant you exchange bodies with another soul. Are souls ready to return this soon?" asked Angie.

"Yes, there are some. You are familiar because you were all walk-ins on Earth I," explained Jeremiel. "We will identify those on

Tenalp who are ready to return to the astral plane. Then we will arrange a walk-in with an appropriate soul."

The group appeared to understand, so he continued, "The ones that appear calm will be the next group to be released to the School of Wisdom. The talkative ones are still a work in progress. They need a little more adjustment time. The most severely damaged souls still have a long therapeutic journey ahead of them."

"What about the souls that come here from Tenalp who don't exchange bodies with a walk-in? Will they come to the resting area too?" asked Angie.

"Yes, they will. Some may need more time in the resting area than others. They will analyze the steps they have made toward improving their karma and then work out future soul enrichment plans. Now come with me. We will enter here and speak to one of the available counselors."

Jeremiel led the way to an area and introduced everyone to an angel who had just ended a session with a confrontational soul. "Please explain to our guests the type of dialogue and questions you were dealing with."

"This particular one believes he has restored love in his soul. But he wants to know more about his own future. I have tried to explain to him that there is a time for everything. Those who are too focused on themselves have not found the loving path. He will resume his required resting time and return to me, time and again, until he is ready."

"What about the most severely damaged souls? Will they be ready any time soon?" asked Angie timidly.

Jeremiel quickly jumped in to field this question. "No, those souls believe that they have done no wrong, and they argue that they shouldn't be here. They truly believe they love everyone when, in reality, they love themselves above all else. They will rest and be counseled and will repeat that cycle over and over again. It will be a very long time before they are ready."

"Can we witness what a conversation with them is like?" asked Angie.

"Sure. Follow me," Jeremiel said as he thanked the angel they were leaving.

They traveled down another corridor and into a room where they found an available angel. "Before you invite your next soul in, my group would like permission to witness your interaction. Can we let them stay behind this divider while you converse? We probably won't stay very long. They just want to get a preview."

"Yes. That would be acceptable. I will summon the next soul."

A very combative soul came upon the scene. We all know someone who thought they were better than and knew more than everyone else. They witnessed this soul argue that he was here too long, was ready to move on, that he understood his wrongdoings, and what he must do to make things right. When the angel asked him what he planned to do to make things right, he mentioned how he would make other souls understand that he had a great deal of knowledge, and they would be wise to listen to him.

Angie made a face, and Jeremiel motioned them to follow him out the back door. When they were out of hearing range, Angie said, "That soul hasn't learned anything."

"Now I can see the stark difference between loving yourself as opposed to loving all souls," commented Mary.

Jeremiel announced, "That was one of the more severely damaged of all souls. Many followed him down the negative path.

Not only is he far from being rehabilitated, but he would poison other souls who have recently found their way back onto the loving path. Let's go to the Meet-and-Greet area. I will meet you there in the morning for our trip to the School of Wisdom."

"Thank you for all your help," acknowledged Angie.

He left them with the unicorns and wished them, "Goodnight."

Chapter 29 – Research at the School of Wisdom

They enjoyed a delightful afternoon and evening. The unicorns nuzzled their friends, affectionately returning the outpouring of affection. The Buffet Hall didn't disappoint, and they found time to discuss their experiences between mouthfuls.

"I'm so glad that there are different phases which souls must successfully complete and that they must find love of others before they are allowed to come to Tenalp," stated Angie.

"I wonder if we will recognize any of them?" asked Mary.

"I doubt it. The incarnating souls will go through the Veil of Forgetfulness and will have a different aura about them, but then again, maybe we will recognize some of them," replied Andrew.

"Let's finish up eating and retire to our chalets. I can't wait to hold you in my arms, my love, and snuggle on the porch and later by the fire," mused Andrew.

Angie reached for his hand in a loving caress. Unable to wait any longer, Andrew and Angie found themselves sitting on the porch swing, watching the setting sun melt into the iridescent pathway left by the rising moon.

The following morning, after much stretching and yawning, they made their way to the Buffet Hall, where they found Matthew and Mary already enjoying their breakfast.

Blueberry pancakes with blueberry compote, thought Angie as a yummy dish appeared before her. She noticed Andrew had wished for the same.

Jeremiel made his entrance as they were finishing up. "It is time to go to the School of Wisdom. We have much to do before Archangel Michael comes to escort you back to the spacecraft."

Please remind us, requested Angie, "How can we move between the Astral Plane and spacecraft so easily?"

"On Earth II, you were all bestowed with a special gift that allows you to come here whenever you desire while others may only visit during their sleep state," explained Jeremiel.

"Of yes," Angie recalled. We have done it so often we don't think about it and take it for granted. It helps to get things back in proper perspective."

"Let us be off," Jeremiel said as he enfolded his enormous wings around them and effortlessly transported them to the School of Wisdom.

This is always a magical place, recollected Angie. Precious stones of every color reflected off the sunlight peeking in through the windows encircling the rotunda. Archangel Jeremiel directed them to an area where they could hold private meetings with some counselors.

Jeremiel explained. "The repentant candidates spent exhaustive hours researching the paths that the loving souls have traveled during prior incarnations. This knowledge helps them to establish wise future choices. The council reviewed, altered, and approved their plans. Aggressive plans designed to repair karma rapidly are rejected in favor of plans that are more likely to result in achievable goals. To explain some specific cases, we have invited a counselor here to speak to you."

A counselor entered the room. She was not breathtakingly beautiful, like the Archangels. She did not hold a pointer like those in charge of the Tapestry Room and Library. She looked quite ordinary in the purity of her white garments. "We do not wear adornments because the focus is not on us. We do not introduce ourselves with names or titles, for that would be distracting. At this stage of the soul's journey, they have completed their stay in the resting area and have demonstrated they are ready to incarnate."

She paused and, sensing no questions, proceeded, "These souls go through several levels here. They sit with counselors to understand how to map out a plan to repair their karma. The School of Wisdom is brimming with resources. They can review the lives of others and select comfortable paths. When the satisfactory plan is developed, the Archangels must consent."

"When a plan is approved, is that when you decide if the soul will be born or be a walk-in?" asked Angie.

"Yes. If a soul doesn't need to benefit from birthing and childhood experiences, they may be allowed to 'walk-in' to a time when they can actively start working on repairing their karma. They will not remember their plans. However, the love overflowing in their hearts should keep them on the loving path.

"I have a couple of meetings for you to observe. One approved plan is a walk-in who will switch with another soul who is ready to return to the Astral Plane. He reviewed all the minute details of the soul's body he is taking over. I must ask that you remain silent and reserve your comments for later."

The counselor began the session. "Welcome. We have observers with us today but don't pay attention to them. As you are aware, your plan is approved, and we have found the perfect situation for you."

The soul listened intently without questions. *That must be further proof that he is ready to accept his future,* thought Angie.

She hadn't spoken a word but soon realized that the others, including the counselor and soul, had heard her. She turned off her thoughts for the moment.

The counselor said, "There is a young man who has been living on Tenalp with a physical handicap. He has worked extremely hard to overcome his handicap with grace and tenacity. It is time for him to return here and draft a new plan for his future incarnation. You have already reviewed this soul's history, specifically his time on Tenalp. You have also expressed a desire to have a physical handicap. Is that true?"

"Yes, that is very true. I will work diligently to master the challenges that face me."

"Good. Now let's show our observers, who know the residents of Tenalp very well, a real-time video of the soul's body that you will take over."

The video played before them. Angie was first to remark, "I know him. We all know him. He has been nice and helpful despite his hardships. We wish you well continuing with his legacy."

"Thank you. I hope to be worthy."

"You will proceed with your walk-in tomorrow night, during the sleep state."

He said his goodbyes and left. The counselor turned toward the guests, looking for comments or questions.

"That reminds me of when we all walked-in on Earth II. We had specific plans, which included each other and our parents," remarked Angie, to which the others agreed.

"The other soul I have invited to join us has just submitted his first draft of a plan. Let's see what he is proposing."

"Welcome. We have some visitors today. Please tell us about your plans."

"I would like to repair my karma as quickly as possible, so I would like to be born small and weak, experiencing the trials and tribulations of childhood through to adult life. I propose a lonely life too. How does that sound?"

"Admirable. However, you have put too much on yourself for this lifetime. These challenges are monumental. You are setting yourself up for failure. Now go back and modify your plans. Perhaps dying alone and lonely is something that you can put off until a future incarnation. Although you may be in a hurry to make amends, we do not want you to fail. Slow and steady will yield success. Come back when you have another plan for us to review."

The soul departed, and Jeremiel stepped forward, "You have given us two practical examples of the incarnation process. We must go now. Thank you for your time and assistance."

Archangel Michael had joined them and swept them up in his mighty wings to travel to the Astral Room on the spacecraft where he addressed them, "How were your visits? You have experienced some of these stages of development personally. Seeing the other side provides an enlightening perspective."

Angie figured he was addressing her, and she replied, "thank you for giving us this opportunity. I was apprehensive, but now I, I mean we, understand more about the process. It will be interesting to watch the one soul walk-in and observe how he does. When a child is born, we will wonder if it is the other soul we met today."

Michael commented, "Today was a learning experience you won't forget. It will enrich your understanding of dealing with the people of Tenalp. Tomorrow, I have a special Archangel for you to meet to allay your fears and concerns further. Until we meet again, I bid you goodnight."

Legna seemed to appear the moment Michael departed. "Welcome back. The time is yours until we meet tomorrow morning. I'll be on the observation deck if you need me."

Angie knew he was inviting her without personally addressing her. He probably felt they should pick up from their last conversation.

"I want to do some research in the Communication Center, advised Mary. "Anyone want to come?"

"Andrew, want to join me in the Multipurpose Room and play some more multi-dimensional chess?" asked Matthew.

"Sure, if Angie doesn't mind."

"I don't mind at all. I'll catch up with everyone later," Angie remarked as she made her way to the Observation Deck, where she found Legna waiting for her.

"Come in," invited Legna as Angie followed him through the opening in the wall. "After our last conversation, I wanted to check in with you. How was your trip?"

"It was excellent. In the resting area, we saw various stages of souls. Some souls were progressing while others were not."

"Now, you must have increased your level of confidence in the process."

"Yes, I did. It is true and comforting. Michael said he has another Archangel for us to meet tomorrow that will further increase our comfort level. I must say I feel better, but I still don't trust the evil souls that ruined Earth I with their selfish ways. At least I know it will be a long time before they are allowed to incarnate on Tenalp."

"I'm glad you had the opportunity. You know I am always available for you."

"Thank you. You are a special friend, Legna. Now I'll be off to meet Mary and maybe say 'Hello' to your sons."

Chapter 30 – Good vs Evil: Featuring Archangel Phanuel

They awoke to the sound of Legna's voice amid the wind chimes. "You will be working with Archangels today. After you get something to eat, please meet me in the Astral Room.

"I wonder who will be working with us? Archangel Michael said it was someone new. I wonder who?" asked Angie.

"We will soon find out," replied Andrew. "Let's get going, sleepyhead."

Archangel Michael met them at the Astral Room entrance. Inside they found the gazebo they loved. Michael was dressed in his royal blue robes and holding his sword, which signified he meant business. As they entered and took their seats, stars filled the room along with a magenta sunset.

"Oh, wow," explained Angie. "Here come, Orion and Mariel!"

Archangel hugs were exchanged to everyone's delight.

"Please take your seats and settle down. We have much information to cover today," announced Michael.

Before he was able to continue, Angie blurted out, "May I ask a question?"

Getting a nod from Archangel Michael, she continued. "I love all the new Archangels we have met—Orion, Mariel, Manakel, Barachiel, Nathaniel, and Ariana. I can see the plan unfolding. But what happens when someone cannot be nudged down the loving path? Is there a judge and jury or some form of government that administers a punishment?"

Archangel Michael was quick to suppress that notion. "Souls will judge themselves when they reach the astral plane. If people learn to live together in harmony, there will be no need for a ruler or leader to enforce planetary laws."

The group nodded their understanding, so Archangel Michael continued, "The next Archangel you will meet has a dual personality. He is gentle and kind, but when confronted with evil, he becomes bright red and smites it out of existence. Understanding the duties of this Archangel will reassure you that any evil that makes it down to the planet's surface and tries to influence any souls will meet their match."

"That is reassuring news," agreed Angie.

"Archangel Phanuel will arrive shortly. He is known as the Angel of Peace, Repentance, and Hope, a heavenly guide. He records, in the Akashic Record Book, every evil that souls have ever encountered. In short, his responsibility is to guide and watch over those who seek eternal life and to protect them from evil spirits."

"You said he has a dual personality. What about his other side?" asked Angie.

"Patience, my dear. His second side is the Archangel of Judgment but in the broadest sense of the word. He sees the errors of peoples' ways and guides them toward the loving path with the help of other Archangels.

Angie looked at Michael with pleading eyes, begging to be able to ask another question.

Michael acknowledged her and she says, "This Archangel who is the Angel of Judgment sounds frightening. What does he do to people who do not behave?"

Michael reminded her, "First, he is the Archangel of Peace. He is like a favorite uncle who loves all his charges and will tolerate much with great patience. That is his gentle blue side, who you will meet shortly. The red side fights evil. He will not allow malice to enter any souls or the astral plane, in which case he becomes the Angel of Exorcism.

"An affected soul may return to the astral plane to rejuvenate itself but never for punishment. Or the soul may choose to stay because once the evil is removed, the soul may go on with its approved plan. All souls will have a chance at eternal life. It is the evil that tries to influence an unsuspecting soul, like an alter ego. It is eradicated without mercy. Let's meet this loving but complex Archangel."

The gentle sound of fluttering wings caught their attention. Michael looked toward the heavens, and they followed his gaze. Amid Orion's stars and Mariel's magenta sunset, a beautiful patch of blue slid toward them. A lamenting cooing accompanied an Archangel. Snow-white doves were perched on his arms and shoulders, flapping their wings in time to the gentle breezes they flew in on.

Angie noticed that he appeared to have enormous eyes but not as large as some of the aliens she had met. At second glance, she realized they weren't that large at all. He was wide-eyed, appearing to take in everything around him. When she looked into his eyes, she was captured by his gaze. The mesmerizing, beautiful shade of blue drew her in like a moth to a flickering flame. He gently raised his arms, and the doves flew up to perch in the rafters. The colorful flower garland, cascading from above, included pansies with their blue faces surrounded by yellow bonnets, bobbing their heads in the wind. Peace lilies were woven into an intricate halo above his head.

His robe was pale blue, signifying calm. Mounds of blue hydrangea bushes encircled the perimeter of their seats.

He spoke not a word. Spellbound and speechless, they walked trance-like into his winged embrace and then returned to their seats. He bowed toward Orion with a glint in his eye that spoke volumes that only those two could understand. "Mariel, my friend, who nudges souls forward along the path of love, great to see you. You make my tasks so much easier. Thank you, Michael, thank you for that ceremonious introduction. Surely I'm not worthy of such accolades."

Archangel Michael commented, "Modesty is one of your endearing qualities. Please continue."

"There are only two things for which I am ultimately concerned: good and evil. When some souls don't respond to Mariel's prodding, I come upon the scene. I will nudge until I am blue in the face, so excuse the color reference. I'm friendly, fun-loving, and, hopefully, someone everyone enjoys being around. Everyone except the evil that sneaks into an unsuspecting soul. Don't confuse evil with negativity that can be dealt with. Evil must be eliminated. I will be merciless. You will see me turn red with determination to slay all evil to the point of exorcism. I will never permit it to enter the astral plane. It will be smitten at the door."

"Angie?" asked Archangel Michael. "Do you understand the difference between negativity that can be redirected toward the loving path and evil which must be removed?"

"Yes, but what happened on Earth when the certain souls became dictators and cared nothing about anybody else but themselves. Why wasn't that negativity redirected or that evil removed?"

"You are very perceptive. There are limitations regarding what we can do. On Earth I, there was free will. People were given a choice, and many veered off the loving path. They were nudged, but multitudes chose to follow the wave of negativity.

"On Earth II, souls achieved a higher vibration giving them free will but only over loving choices. On Tenalp, they have free will from infancy with guidance from the angels. In time, they will learn not to follow anything harmful or hurtful.

"We must also keep in mind that all souls make their life plans and map out their life purposes before they incarnate. Specific objectives cannot be changed. If someone chooses to live in poverty, to have an illness, or suffer a disaster to learn a life lesson to enrich their soul, that choice cannot be altered.

"At times, a generation will be granted a teaching. If many souls select the type of life where they will be given the choice of living a loving life versus a selfish, greedy life, their request will be answered on a large scale. On Earth I, selected souls were allowed to lead with cruelty in plain sight, thus giving other souls the chance to choose the loving path. It was never the intention for the leaders of the mass teaching to turn dark. They were required to keep love in their hearts while they gave others choices.

"Over time, the teachers became arrogant criminals who divided souls, ridiculed their differences, and took away the planet's protections. They no longer offered a free will choice. Instead, they led their flock down a very dark path, and many could not work their way back.

"You were there. It became so horrendous that you had to rescue the loving souls to let Earth I implode and be replaced by the new planet Earth. Even sending down a deadly virus did not bring people together. Those who were blinded by their self-importance are the ones spending a long time in the resting area.

Archangel Michael wrapped it up by saying, "I have explained the three elements: free will, predetermined life plans, and generational plans. Archangel Phanuel, do you have any final thoughts to add?

"The Generational plan for Tenalp is to learn to live in love. Any negativity will be redirected. All evil will be exorcised. I can see all and will watch the four of you locate souls that are wavering. I will watch Mariel as she nudges souls toward the loving path. We will celebrate the successes. However, if a soul is being pulled in the wrong direction, I will try my methods by protecting them from others' negativity. I will recognize evil and will remove it without hesitation. Do not try to distinguish between negativity and evil. Leave that to me."

"Doesn't that make you the judge?" asked Angie.

"Never a judge. An observer and a heavenly guide toward those who eventually want to inherit eternal life. Remember the Tapestry of Life? Remember the threads that have gone dark, adversely affecting all other souls it came in contact with? Remember the bad souls who turned Earth I into overwhelming negative energy that needed to be destroyed?"

Phanuel sensed the total agreement of those he was addressing. "Good. Evil spreads quickly, and I must remove it from within the soul. If necessary, I whisk away a damaged soul to the resting area."

Angie became lost in her thoughts. *He was such a comfortable sort of angel, like a cool cat to have had such an important job. He was calm, peaceful, and collected to help him decide which souls needed to return to the astral plane for more resting time.*

"Thank you, Angie, for recognizing my talents and mission. My most significant task is to watch over everyone. I walk a fine line as I try to give hope and eradicate all negativity and evil. Souls are good and loving, but some get clouded in their judgment calls, while evil will occasionally take over a soul. It happens. Every soul is worth fighting for, and every evil must be eradicated.

With a nod to the other Archangels, Phanuel issued an invitation, "Come with me and let's observe the children once more, playing gleefully. Their joy and laughter make my heart sing. "

They found themselves on Mount Overlook with Michael, Orion, Mariel, and Phanuel, who continued with his observation. "See the adults watching over the children with smiles on their faces. There is joy in the air. I see no evil. I believe they are ready for the next step toward improving their living conditions."

Orion and Mariel bid them farewell and departed.

Chapter 31 – The Miracle of Water: Featuring Archangel Arariel

I don't like what I see at all," announced Angie. "Michael, I really need to speak to you."

"What is wrong?" asked Phanuel as Michael moved to stand next to him.

"I love seeing children happy and playful. It is music to my ears. Please look closely. They are filthy, their hair is a tangled, dirty mess, and they eat off dirty stones. It is awful, unacceptable. What can be done?"

"Angie, my dear, they are perfectly happy living that way. They don't know of a better way."

"But Michael, they don't have to live this way. They deserve to enjoy a clean life, countered Angie.

"First, let us bid Phanuel farewell. Thank you for meeting us and explaining your mission. Removing evil is extremely important. You must go now and keep the peace." Phanuel departed amid a flurry with the doves of peace.

"Angie, what do you see? What exactly bothers you?" asked Michael

Angie was stunned that she was asked to lead the discussion. She remained silent for a brief moment, collecting her thoughts. "They know how to wash and clean up in the salty water. Look at that girl scooping up handfuls of water from that small stream. She is drinking it and trying to wash herself and her hair in handfuls of water. I understand this is a primitive society, but can't we help them?"

"Yes, we can, Angie, and the time is right," announced Michael

Angie stared at Michael, surprised that she had won her point with no further argument.

"Let's bring our gazebo here to our mountain top observation post. It will remain out of sight, affording us some comfort while we meet our next Archangel."

The gazebo appeared before them just as quickly as the first one had appeared on the astral plane.

"Kindly take your seats. It is time to present the wonders of water to the village," instructed Michael.

Angie had noticed that the gazebo was devoid of flowers and birds when it appeared. At the mention of water, a light rain began to fall, playing a symphony of rhythmic tunes upon the roof. They looked up to see the rafters lined with Water Lilies. An aromatic fragrance wafted down, delighting their noses.

A large water droplet, the size of an enormous snow globe, materialized in the entryway. It tilted and swayed like gelatin. Angie and the others moved back, anticipating a flood if the bubble burst. Inside they could see a majestic Archangel adorned in a red cloak. He held a pitcher in each hand. Iridescent raindrops, sparkling like miniature prisms, encircled his golden locks.

The bubble popped with a splash. Water poured forth from the containers, cascading like waterfalls down the length of his robe.

"Greetings, Archangel Arariel, and welcome to our gathering." He opened his wings, displaying glistening droplets. Michael said, "I see you have heard of the mandatory Archangel hugs. Please proceed, and then we'll get down to business."

No one wanted to get wet. Greetings and hesitant hugs were exchanged.

As they returned to their seats, Angie observed and shared. "Your robe appears to be wet, yet we are dry from our hugs."

"It is all a matter of perspective and visual effects," Arariel stated. "Notice that I am now holding a divining rod and trident. I prefer to hold water jugs within my travel droplet. My rod and staff could appear to poke holes.

"Thank you for the warm welcome. My name is Arariel, and I am the Archangel and patron saint of the waters and everything within them. Together, we will introduce this community to water and its many uses."

"Wonderful," announced Angie, with the others nodding in agreement.

"Water has many cleaning properties. I can assist in washing away negative emotions. I am also known as the Archangel of stupidity."

"Stupidity?" exclaimed Angie. "I've never heard such a thing."

"That is one of my tasks that takes the most explaining. Stupid actions are not malicious. They are non-thinking. I can help cleanse away the brain fog, allowing people to think and act clearly.

"My main focus on Tenalp will be the rivers, streams, tributaries, springs, lakes, ponds, and the seas—all bodies of water. There is a babbling brook near their settlement, which isn't deep. The children enjoy rock hopping, where they get wet and refreshed. It is not deep enough for bathing. It is time to show the villagers how to dam it up."

"If we can't let people see us, how can we do that?" asked Angie.

"It will be quite easy. People return to their cave dwellings when the sun goes down. That is when we get to work and find a place where water can collect. And we will need to fell a tree to dam up the water."

"Good idea!" exclaimed Angie while the others nodded in agreement.

"One log will help the inhabitants figure out how to form a dam for washing, cooking, and bathing. Some will follow the stream to the spring and will find drinking water. Refreshing, clean, salt-free water will be treasured. With the help of Archangel Manakel, the fish will eventually be contained at the mouths of the rivers and streams. In time, fallen tree trunks will be made into canoes. Surf fishing will advance to canoe fishing. Someday they will figure out how to travel by water. You can see how one log can open the door to endless possibilities."

"Are we sure we have curious people among them?"

"We will plant thoughts in the dreams of the creative ones. Their imagination will show them the way. People stumble thru the unknown. Imparting thoughts through dreams has much better results.

Archangel Michael interrupted their conversation. "It is time to go. It will be nightfall soon, and you must select the perfect spot to place the log."

"I have something to do first. Look yonder toward the ocean. I won't be long," announced Arariel as he disappeared.

As they exited the gazebo, it vanished from sight. They could see Arariel swimming with the dolphins to the backdrop of a beautiful sunset. In the distance, a humongous whale and calf could be seen slapping the water with their tails.

Arariel returned and advised, "No one is at the stream, so let's go."

They said goodbye to Michael, held hands with Arariel, and traveled the entire length of the stream. It didn't take long for them to find the perfect spot, with a depression where water would collect nicely. There was a tree that was hit by lightning and was easy to push across the stream. A few rocks to plug up some holes, and they were done for the night.

"That was easy," exclaimed Matthew. "Are we going to stay with Legna tonight? I could use some food, not to mention a stay in the molecular room." The others smiled in agreement.

"Yes," replied Arariel. "Legna is waiting for you." I will see you at the observation post in the morning. Legna will bring you over in the shuttle so that we can remain cloaked as we travel the length of the stream. Have a lovely evening."

The evening was enjoyable, restful, and morning arrived quickly, with Legna appearing at their door while the wind chime alarm played their wake-up song. "Time to get up. We will leave soon."

Anxious to see what had transpired when the villagers found the change to their stream, they were ready in a flash and sitting in the shuttle, ready to go.

Once on the planet, Arariel joined them in the craft, and off they went. They first checked the village and saw a line of people walking toward the stream while others followed the stream bed. Where once water flowed, barely a trickle was visible. One girl, known as Brook, was leading the way, running and tripping over the stones.

"Come here!" she yelled. "I found the water. Look! A log fell and blocked the water, and now we have lots of water. Fantastic!" she exclaimed as she jumped in, making a big splash. Others followed. Soon there were screams of delight as the young ones played while the adults marveled at the sight."

"Success," proclaimed Arariel. We will leave thoughts in their dreams, especially Brook. She is very enthusiastic and will be perfect for the quest to find the spring and other uses for their newfound treasure."

"Can we stay and watch awhile?" asked Angie.

"Sure, if Legna has the time. I must leave you, but I will be returning when water becomes the main focus of the community."

Legna agreed to stay for a little while, and the foursome enjoyed observing the merriment that filled the air.

Chapter 32 – Sky and Stormy:
Featuring Archangel Gadiel

As the days passed and the group spent time observing, Angie noticed a beautiful young woman. Her eyes were the color of a clear blue sky, and her hair was the color of the shimmering sun. Even in a crude wrap-around dress made of braided leaves, she looked stunning. Her graceful gait and feminine gestures accentuated her beauty. As Angie listened closer, she heard someone call out, "Sky."

"Coming!" her voice echoed like a melody. Not a sing-song voice but more like a choir of angels with poise and grace.

"How wonderful!" Angie exclaimed out loud. "What a beautiful vision of loveliness living in this primitive, crude society."

Angie watched an older female putting wood on the fire and speaking so softly to Sky that Angie couldn't hear what they said but could surmise it was a request for help as Sky ran off and started picking up small sticks, probably for the fire.

"*Who is that?*" asked Angie to herself, observing someone coming onto the scene.

Sky came across a young man of about her same age, both young adults. When their eyes met, love and kindness transcended the moment. Sky looked down as the male whispered in her ear. Her cheeks turned bright red as she quickly resumed her task. He went back to work too, but then their hands touched when they reached for the same twig. He released his grasp, allowing her to have it.

"I like this guy," Angie concluded and speaking to no one in particular. "Respectful love."

Later Angie noticed them again. "*Why are they avoiding each other's glances? Is it because they are in the company of others?*"

Angie summoned Archangel Michael. "A male and female with what appears to be a mutual attraction, but they avoid each other in public. She needs guidance. Can I please visit her during her dreamtime and suggest she talk to her guardian angels about this situation?"

"Sure, Angie. Just don't reveal yourself to her. Speak to her guardian angels and request that they intervene as well. Make sure you are not playing matchmaker but instead, you are sincerely interested in helping them on the loving path they seem to be on."

Before sleep time, Angie watched for Sky again. She found her gathering more wood.

"Stormy!" Sky called out in her loving voice. He turned and ran to her side. They almost kissed before Sky turned away.

"We can't keep hiding our love from the others, Sky."

"Stormy, we must! Our parents might object."

"How will we know if they do? My parents have only spoken kind words about you."

"But, but." Sky protested with cheeks burning.

"Are you ashamed to be with me?" He gently placed his bundle of firewood in her arms and walked off as he said, "Have it your way."

Tears welled up in Sky's eyes, spilling down her cheeks.

"I do love him," she cried under her breath. "I'm not ashamed. I'm afraid. What if my parents don't like him? What then? I couldn't live with that!" Sky sobbed out the words while more tears stained the forest floor.

Angie listened, wishing she could console Sky when she saw a Guardian Angel appear next to her. It looked like the angel was comforting her as she whispered to her.

Sky took a deep breath and wiped the tears from her eyes, not realizing she left dirt-stained streaks on her cheeks. Angie watched as she headed back to camp and ran into a father figure.

Angie wondered if this was her Papa.

"What is wrong with your face? Who made you cry?"

"No one Papa. My eyes teared from the sun."

She added her twigs to the fire. Then she returned to the privacy of the forest, where she found a log to sit on.

"What should I do?" she pleaded, cradling her head in her hands.

"Is she calling her Guardian Angel again?" asked Angie.

Emotions clouded Angie's thoughts. *I can't bear to watch her suffering. Archangel Michael, I need you to help me do more.*

"What is it, Angie?" Archangel Michael inquired as he appeared before her once again.

"Sky is so upset. I want to help her!"

Archangel Michael summoned the group who had been observing others. Soon, Andrew, Mary, and Matthew were by Angie's side on the top of Mount Overlook.

Archangel Michael explained to the gathering, "Angie has witnessed a lover's dilemma and wants to help. We cannot interfere. However, guidance during dreamtime is appropriate. It is also a perfect time to introduce you to Archangel Gadiel."

With a flutter of wings, the group looked up to see feathers tipped in shades of brilliant yellow intermittently with shades of green. An Archangel appeared before them. As the winds swirled around him, his gown changed from iridescent shades of yellows to iridescent shades of greens. His aura was also yellow and green, and when he opened his wings, these colors radiated very gently, welcoming them into his arms. Customary archangel hugs were exchanged.

"Hello, my name is Gadiel. Thank you, Archangel Michael, for summoning me as I am most anxious to help. I am the Archangel you call when you have a dilemma and need to make a decision. My colors have significant meaning illuminating my task. The yellow signifies caution, and green indicates go. When people have a problem, they should call out to me before they proceed, the yellow, and I will instruct them, representing go or green.

"Your voice is so beautiful like a Nightingale," complimented Angie.

Gadiel nodded as he continued. "In my hand, you will see a cross. This cross symbolizes the crossroads one can find themselves in. I will show them the way."

"How can you help Sky?" asked Angie

"When someone is feeling down and feels like they are a victim of life's trials and tribulations, they can call on me to protect them and to release any negative feelings, especially after a disagreement or argument with a friend or lover."

"Perfect, but how can we explain you to Sky? We can't invite her here," questioned Angie.

"There are a few ways. One way is for me to speak to her guardian angels. They will gladly intervene on my behalf."

"But it would be so much better if she knew your name and could call on your directly," contended Angie.

"The other way is to enter her dreams and tell her to go outside when the wind is blowing and call my name three times, letting the wind bring her request up toward the heavens. I will reply during her dreamtime."

"Do you want me to tell you what I observed?" offered Angie.

"No. When Sky sends her request to me, I will see what's in her heart and the hearts of those around her."

"How can these people learn about you and all the Archangels? How can they find out who to call on to make a request?" asked Angie, sincerely wanting to help everyone.

"They are familiar with their guardian angels. They will learn to communicate their desires through them. The Archangels are there to help everyone but primarily through the guardian angels."

"Okay," agreed Angie.

Gadiel continued, "Tonight, during her dream state, I will clear the confusing atmosphere with a reflective mirror where she can visualize herself speaking to her Father and Mother and professing her love. She will see their acceptance. Then she will visualize herself with her soulmate as their loving path is illuminated before them. When you return, you will see the happy union of Sky and Storm because they are meant to be together."

A couple of nights later, Angie saw that Sky and Stormy were sitting together, holding hands, for all to see.

"Success! Gadiel came through for us!" Angie announced.

Archangel Michael had joined them, pleased with the outcome. "Remember that we are not here to resolve all situations. If their life's path was not to find love in this lifetime, we could not have done anything. Also, we are not matchmakers. In most instances, the Guardian Angels will work with the Archangels helping to resolve problems. In this case, it was an excellent opportunity for you to meet Archangel Gadiel.

"Come. It will be nightfall soon, and the occupants will return to their caves. You must return to the spacecraft where Legna is waiting for you."

Chapter 33 – Shaken to the Core: Featuring Archangels Gersisa, Christiel & Purlimiek

A booming voice, loud and clear, cut through the quiet sleeping quarters. The foursome had enjoyed a long, tiring day and was soon fast asleep aboard the spacecraft when they heard, "Wake up quick and get down to the Astral Meeting Room without delay." It was Archangel Michael's voice, which made them bolt into action.

Trying to unwrap themselves from their tangled bedding and tripping as they tried to jump into their clothes, they rushed to the Astral Room onboard the craft. They found Archangel Michael and Legna standing on either side of a beautiful Archangel whom they had never seen before. As she moved, her robes transformed from flawless steel gray to a sparkly silver. Through diamond-like prisms that radiated around the room, you could see her silver crown studded with diamonds. She exuded power with elegant grace. The group was momentarily mesmerized.

Without waiting for an introduction or offering any archangel hugs, this stunning Archangel spoke in a calm yet urgent manner.

"I am Archangel Gersisa, and I have command over the Inner Earth. An earthquake has frightened the community." As she stepped aside, a screen revealed the chaos in real time.

People were fleeing hither and yon like a disturbed anthill. They were running out of the caves only to be met with an aftershock when they immediately turned on their heels and fled back into the caves. A few moments later, they were running back out as if they had seen a ghost. Their screams pierced the air with utter terror.

Angie, with a wild look in her eyes, demanded, "How did this happen?"

"There is no time to explain. Right now, I need you to get down there immediately. Archangel Christiel is at Mount Overlook right now. She will explain how you can help. Meanwhile, I must calm the inner Earth. Archangels Selaphiel, the Archangel of the Planets, and Archangel Butyalil, the Archangel in charge of the planet's delicate balance, are waiting for me. I promise, when the situation is under control, we will return with a full explanation." As she was turning to leave, she paused and added, "Upon our return, we will exchange archangel hugs. Please hurry. Archangel Christiel is waiting for you."

Archangels Michael and Gersisa were gone in a flash. The group held tight to Legna's hands and was instantly at Mount Overlook. They were stunned into silence as they observed nervousness, anxiousness, and breathlessness all rolled up into an absolute panic. There was an unknown threat to the very heart of their colony. Another tremble reverberated from deep below the ground. The colonists ran from the shelter of the caves back outside, where more tremors greeted them in the shadowy darkness. Branches shook and rattled furiously, and tree limbs cracked. The forest-dwelling creatures were racing from some unknown demon. The exiting human stampede abruptly turned and again ran back into the cave, hoping to find shelter.

Unfortunately, their 'shelter' was anything but. The shaking intensified within the confined space while the noise reverberated off the walls. Adults and children were crying and weeping uncontrollably. They didn't know what was happening or how to escape.

"We have work to do," Legna said.

He broke their stunned trance. They turned to witness an Archangel with her enormous wings spread out over the village, emitting a golden, calming mist over the crowd. Now the occupants seemed to be running in slow motion. At that same time, the trembling seemed to slow down. As the golden mist filled the air and drifted down upon the villagers, they turned their gaze toward the skies in wide-eyed wonder. They did not see the angel wings that protected them. Her calming warm light had replaced the darkness with the most beautiful sunrise anyone could have ever imagined. Their panic dissolved.

"Is it over?" asked Angie.

"Maybe." The beautiful golden Archangel had spoken and drew their attention. "I am Archangel Christiel. I am sending down peace and love dissolving all negativity and confusion." A brilliant light encircled her angelic form from head to toe. Her golden robes shimmered with gold dust, and her halo was illuminated with sparklers exploding with a glow radiating in all directions.

"These people have no idea what is going on," interrupted Angie.

"Archangel Gersisa is working below in the depths of the planet. She will explain in more detail later."

"How can we help?" asked Angie and Mary simultaneously.

"Welcome, Archangel Purlimiek." To everyone's wonder, Archangel Christiel was addressing another Archangel who, at the mention of his name, came upon the scene with a flash. His robes, halo, and entire aura flooded the area with a pale soft blue-green light contrasting with the golden mist. "I am the Archangel of Nature with an emphasis on harmony and healing. I need your help finding some calming woods to burn in their campfires."

"What's a calming wood?" asked Angie.

"Let's start with what we know. Nature has been threatened with the earthquake. Archangel Gersisa is calming this planet's internal workings while Archangel Christiel has brought forth her calming mist. Now, we must bring continuing calm to the inhabitants—people, animals, insects, and birds."

Archangel Purlimiek continued, "I'm sure you have heard of Sandalwood, Frankincense, Patchouli, and Chamomile. If we can infuse the area with these, we can infuse the community with peace. Sandalwood is one of the most mind-calming fragrances, and it comes from mature, 15-20-year-old Sandalwood trees. We never cut down the tree. Instead, we will look for a recently fallen tree branch with signs of life in it. When the branches burn on their fires, the Sandalwood fragrance gives forth a calm aura. The ashes have a long-lasting effect, so one tree limb will be fine for now."

"That sounds wonderful. Can you help us find this tree? Is there anything else that will help them?" asked Angie in her typical multi-questioning but sincerely helpful style.

"Yes, I will help you find the Sandalwood tree limbs. And I will guide you to the large fragrant furry leaves of the Patchouli plant. We will add them to the fires as well. Then, I will help you find the small daisy-like flowers on the Chamomile plant. We will encourage the residents to put them in hot water to drink as tea. Finally, we will collect tears of Frankincense."

"That sounds wonderful," exclaimed Mary. "When can we go?"

"Wait. What are tears of Frankincense?" asked Angie.

"It is best to show you the tears. The sooner we leave, the better. While we are wandering the countryside searching for these ingredients, we will come across Archangel Fhelyai. He is the

Archangel over the animals and nature. He is calming the woodland creatures that have been running for the hills. He will help us signal the birds. We will follow their calls."

Archangel Purlimiek enfolded his mighty wings around them, and they found themselves in a beautiful meadow. Within the collective conscience of their minds, they heard their guide summon forth Archangel Fhelyai.

Chapter 34 – Calming Sandalwood: Featuring Archangel Fhelyai

A sunny yellow Archangel appeared before them. Rays of sunbeams bounced from his aura, bathing the field in warming sunlight. His staff was a gentle sunbeam. A sunny smile lit his face. "This is Archangel Fhelyai, our Archangel of Nature with dominion over the animals and the plant life. What are the conditions down here after the earthquake?"

Archangel Fhelyai explained, "The animals were frightened, and I have been whispering calming words of peace on the gentle breezes. Some plants have been shaken loose, and I have reminded them to extend their roots back down into the Earth as far as they can go. My radiant sunlight is encouraging their flowery faces to look up toward me and be nurtured by my rays."

"That sounds wonderful. I'm Angie, and I'd like to introduce you to Andrew, Mary, and Matthew. We are here to help, and Archangel Purlimiek is taking us to find Sandalwood and other calming ingredients for the community. Let us know if we can help you too."

"Before you go, will you call the birds and ask them to lead the way in song?" Archangel Purlimiek asked Archangel Fhelyai.

"Absolutely. I certainly appreciate your willingness to help, and I will remember your offer. Meanwhile, I must get back to the business at hand, which is calming all of nature." With that statement, Archangel Fhelyai departed, leaving sunshine in his wake with bird calls filling the air.

"He is so nice," stated Mary.

"Yes, I hope we get to meet him again and some of the animals under his care," Angie said.

"I'm sure we will be calling out to him again real soon," stated Archangel Purlimiek. "For now, I need your help getting a Sandalwood limb close to the community. Let's find the perfect branch, and then I will need your help carrying it. I don't want the people to see us. The guardian angels will encourage some of the strongest to find the branch and drag it in to lay on the fire. Then we will go find the other ingredients."

"How will we find the Sandalwood trees in this thick foliage?" asked Angie.

"We will follow the songs from above. Archangel Fhelyai has asked the Starlings and Koel birds to help us."

"But how?" continued Angie.

"First, we will look up to the skies for the graceful undulating flight of a flock of Starlings. We will hear their sound like waves breaking on the shoreline. They will swoop back and forth, hovering over the Sandalwood Grove. As we get closer, we will listen for the Koel birds' cry, who will call out to us. Their cry sounds like, "Hey, yo." They love the Sandalwood trees and will bring us right to them."

"There are the Starlings. Look up! They are flying with amazing precision. Look at how they turn on a dime and don't bump into each other. Let's follow them," announced Angie.

"Yes. Let us follow the Starlings," agreed Archangel Purlimiek, "and start listening for the call of the Koel bird who will be perching in the Sandalwood trees."

Angie had grabbed hold of Andrew's hand so she could look up but keep a steady footing. Mary and Matthew followed them also hand in hand with eyes peering toward the heavens.

"Hear that?" asked Angie. They all stopped and listened. The sound of the Starlings had subsided, and now, a bird was calling out. "Well, I'll be. It does sound like that bird is yelling, 'Hey yo.' Hurry."

As they got closer and closer, the foliage changed. There was calm in the air. The smell of the woodlands had changed to Sandalwood. The feathery leaves gently waved on the breezes as if conducting an orchestra.

Archangel Purlimiek explained, "Those are the leaves of the Sandalwood trees. We must now find a branch separated from a tree. Perhaps the earthquake shook some loose, and we can find one that still has the life force within."

"How about this one?" asked Andrew, pointing toward a good-sized tree limb but not too large for them to carry.

"That is perfect. We must also collect some seed pods from the Sandalwood tree and some from the Wattles tree. They grow best together. See those long hanging pods. They are from the Wattles, and we are permitted to take them without doing damage to the tree."

Before long, they had their pockets full of seed pods, and all four of them had grabbed hold of the Sandalwood limb and started on their way back through the forest.

"It is surprising how light this limb is considering how long it is," remarked Mary.

"The wood of the Sandalwood is not dense and, therefore, quite light. We will be able to get the limb back before nightfall. The plan is to leave it outside the village community to be discovered by those looking for firewood," explained Archangel Purlimiek.

Having completed their task, Archangel Purlimiek bid them farewell saying, "We will meet again tomorrow and go in search of the other calming essentials. Archangel Fhelyai will help guide us again."

No sooner had Purlimiek vanished, Legna approached them, grabbed hands, and whisked them back to the ship.

After some food, they settled down in their beds. Angie mentally shared her prayer for the night, "I pray the village is calm and the earthquakes have stopped. I'm anxious to see the village and the Archangels in the morning. Goodnight."

No one was hungry in the morning, so they asked Legna to get them down to the Mount Overlook without delay. There they found Archangel Christiel with her enormous wings spread out over the village, continuing to emit the golden, calming mist but to a much lesser degree.

"Good morning," announced Archangel Christiel. "Thank you for bringing the limb of the Sandalwood tree. They have found it and added some to their fires. I can already see the benefits, so I was able to reduce my calming mist. By tomorrow morning, after you complete the day's tasks, I will be able to discontinue the mist."

"What are our tasks?" asked Angie.

Chapter 35 – Butterfly Fields

With a flash of blue-green light, Archangel Purlimiek greeted them, "Hello and a wonderful job we did yesterday finding the Sandalwood tree limb. The mother tree was not disturbed and will continue to provide her medicinal properties for years to come. As the Archangel of Nature, I am responsible for keeping the balance on this new planet. That tree will continue to thrive for another 50 years."

"I'm sure I can speak for all of us when I say we enjoyed the entire experience, and we're delighted to help the village. The people have become very dear to us," said Angie. "And of course, we understand the importance of your role in nature after witnessing the destruction of the original planet Earth."

With the others in agreement, Archangel Purlimiek continued, "It is time to go and meet up with Archangel Fhelyai again. He will be your guide to finding and gathering the final ingredients."

They joined hands and transported to a beautiful field just beyond the village. Birds were chirping and flying from tree to tree like acrobats on the wind. Flowers were bobbing their colorful heads everywhere. Butterflies graced the field with their brilliant cloaks. Bees were working their pollinating magic after the earthquake disruption, which had affected all living creatures.

"It is absolutely beautiful here," exclaimed Mary. "It is the type of place I would love to have a picnic and rest and enjoy the beauty."

"Yes, I agree," stated Archangel Fhelyai, who startled them with his brilliant sunny appearance that blended in with their surroundings.

Archangel Purlimiek acknowledged Archangel Fhelyai with a nod and announced, "It is time for me to leave you to your tasks, for which I again thank you. We will meet again soon."

"Mary, I heard your wish that you would love to enjoy this gorgeous field. I have a surprise for you. Take your seats on the grasses. You will not hurt them." Archangel Fhelyai motioned for them to take a seat.

"We have three calming items to bestow on the village, Frankincense, Patchouli, and Chamomile. I would like to explain a little about each of them. Then we will plan to gather these treasures just before nightfall so we can leave the fresh ingredients at the campfires when the villagers have retired into the caves for the night."

"Sounds like it will be a late night, and we didn't have any breakfast. Will we have time to eat something somewhere?" asked Matthew.

"How did that get here?" asked Angie as she answered her own question. "Oh, yes. Just like the gazebo appeared before our eyes in the Meet-and-Greet area. The Archangels can make almost anything happen."

A red and white blanket with a couple of wicker picnic baskets appeared before them. Without being asked, Matthew opened and started emptying the contents. There were four labeled vegetable salad containers with lettuce, tomatoes, mushrooms, peppers, onions, and chickpeas, depending on their tastes.

"Oh, good," remarked Angie. Mine has no onions and peppers.

"And mine has extra mushrooms and no chickpeas," remarked Mary.

Andrew and Matthew took no notice of their contents and dug right in.

Finishing quickly, Matthew handed out labeled containers of fruit salad. There was water for all.

"Enjoy your feast," proclaimed Archangel Fhelyai. "While you finish, I will explain about the plants we are here to harvest."

"We will start with Frankincense, which is the resin of the scraggly Boswellia Tree. The tree is easy to spot and grows in the woodsy areas surrounding these fields. They can grow out of rocks and other unforgiving places too. The bark easily peels down in circular strips, bouncing like a yoyo on the breezes."

"Look at that beautiful colorful tree that has the same coloring as Monarch Butterflies," Angie pointed out.

Mary added, "And that tree is iridescent blue."

With a whistle from Archangel Fhelyai, the Monarch Butterfly tree took to flight. Millions of Monarch butterflies circled the tree, rising higher and higher, obscuring all clouds in the sky. They danced on the winds and circled the field, putting on an elaborate show. After a few moments, they settled back down on the tree branches giving the appearance of leaves.

With a second whistle from Archangel Fhelyai, the iridescent blue tree unraveled as thousands of blue butterflies circled higher and higher and then danced around the fields. After their breath-taking show, they also settled on the tree branches without so much as a flutter.

"Wow. What a stunning display. They are gorgeous. I have never seen so many butterflies. It is like a symphony of radiant colors," remarked Angie.

Archangel Fhelyai said, "look beyond to some other trees. Do you notice anything?

"I see! Look!" exclaimed Angie as she pointed to some of the curled ribbon bark.

"You have correctly identified the Boswellia Tree," confirmed Archangel Fhelyai. "Beneath the bark, you will see hardened streaks of resin called tears. When steamed, the tears give off a woody, spicy smell. The aroma, when absorbed through the skin, offers healing and calming properties. You can also spot them by their little white flowers with yellow buds that open to reveal a red center."

"Tears make it sound like the tree is crying," said Mary with a frown upon her face.

"Don't worry, Mary. The tree sheds its bark, and the tears symbolize the tears of those that are frightened. They are the tree's calming tears to remove the fears."

Mary's frown turned upside down at Archangel Fhelyai's words, so he continued, "You will gather tears, and tonight, when everyone is asleep in their caves, you will place them on the rocks surrounding the fire. Don't take them all. You will leave some tears on the trees so they will know how to find more." The group nodded in agreement.

"The next plant I would like to introduce to you is the Patchouli. It releases its calming properties when subjected to steam. The plants are bushy and look like mint with large fragrant furry leaves and small pale pink-white flowers. There is a patch of Patchouli plants over there," directed Archangel Fhelyai as he pointed them out. "You will lay the leaves on the rocks surrounding the fire along with the Frankincense tears. The Villagers will like the decorative look and will continue with the practice. The Guardian Angels will encourage them by placing that thought in their minds. They might eventually make it into a tea, eat it as a vegetable or use it as a seasoning. Patchouli is an anti-depressant and is used to treat anxiety, nervousness, and exhaustion.

"It is amazing how many wonderful properties these trees and plants have hidden within. Thank you for explaining. Perhaps we can share this information with the new Earth," suggested Angie.

"It is my understanding that there is no illness on the new Earth, and there is no need to eat for nourishment. The water contains all the nutrients people need. However, they can enjoy these plants for the taste and aroma."

"Yes, you are right," agreed Angie.

"Finally, I would like to tell you about the Chamomile plants which are over there. They look like Daisies. The Guardian angels will encourage the villagers to add them to hot water to drink as tea. They may come to enjoy chamomile in their foods or use it as a mouthwash. Skin salve can be made from a cooled tea compress. We will gather some leaves for them."

"This is wonderful information, and we are thrilled to help. Thank you so much for giving us the opportunity," stated Angie.

"My pleasure. The villagers have already learned that the gel in Aloe leaves can calm burns. It is time to increase their knowledge of the other plants that grow naturally and contain healing properties. Your help has made this possible. Angels needed your hands to carry the Sandalwood log and now, to gather and arrange the tears and flowers around the fire."

"It is mid-day, and the children may be wandering into this field. We will meet again later, so I can guide you through the collection and distribution. It is time for you to return to the spacecraft for some rest."

He took their hands, and off they went to Mount Overlook, where they found Legna waiting. Legna took Fhelyai's place in the circle, and off they went to the spacecraft.

Chapter 36 – Inner Planet:
Featuring the Return of Archangel Gersisa

Back onboard the craft, Angie, Andrew, Matthew & Mary found it impossible to settle down. They had so much to talk about. Laem invited them to the dining area, where they continued their conversations, impolitely, with their mouths full. No rest for their active minds.

Nightfall crept over the valley. Since they needed some light to find their ingredients, Legna quickly escorted them to Mount Overlook. Archangel Fhelyai switched places with Legna, enveloped the group in his magnificent Archangel wings, and transported them down to the field they had visited earlier that afternoon. This Archangel's rays of sunlight bathed the fields in a warming glow. His staff of gentle sunbeams was useful as the shadows grew taller over the land. His sunny smile illuminated his face.

They split up, and under his watchful eye, they gathered Frankincense tears, Patchouli leaves, and the Chamomile flowers. Stealthily they entered the village square and quietly arranged the calming elements around the campfire.

They could hear Archangel Fhelyai whisper, "Well done," as they transported back to Mount Overlook. He gave them archangel hugs and departed, taking the last rays of sunlight with him. Legna, who had been waiting for them, took their hands, and they returned to the spacecraft.

It has been a long but satisfying day, and soon they were snug in their beds and lost in dreamland. They didn't even have enough energy to meander down to the kitchen.

Legna announced daybreak with the pleasant sound of the wind chimes. After waterless misting showers, they dressed, not knowing the perfect attire of the day. Yesterday, they had dressed for the outdoors. Today was still a mystery, so they dressed casually, always wearing the pins Wendy had given them. Legna escorted them to Mount Overlook, where they met Archangel Gersisa, whom they had briefly met a couple of days earlier when the earthquake shook the planet to its very core.

Angie marveled at Gersisa's appearance. As she moved toward them, ready to bestow archangel hugs, they once again witnessed her robes transform from flawless steel gray to a sparkly silver. Diamond-like prisms radiated around the room and were complemented by her silver crown, studded with diamonds.

"It is nice to see you all again," announced Archangel Gersisa. "I have communicated with Archangels Christiel, Purlimiek, and Fhelyai. They applaud you for the help you delivered to the community. As you can see, Christiel's calming energy rays are no longer needed. She has left to attend to other duties thanks to the success of your mission.

"Now, as I promised, I will explain my role. My command is over the Inner planet. I am bestowed with the gift of white fingers of light that I can send deep into the planet to restore balance." As she spoke, she twilled her fingers before them, capturing their attention."

"How can you do that?" asked Angie.

"Don't let looks deceive you. There is magnificent power in my small fingers," Archangel Gersisa continued, speaking with a depth and feeling that ignited their minds.

"You have studied plants and solar systems. Let's visualize. Imagine our universe with heavy globes of all sizes, moving around a sun while staying in their assigned places. Now ask yourself how this could be possible. The spheres are all different weights and dimensions and are composed of various volatile materials. The key is what is inside the globes and how to harness and contain that energy.

"To better understand the working of the inner planet, I have invited someone you know very well."

An Archangel drifted onto the scene, surrounded by twinkling stars. They watched him enter with the folds of his midnight blue velvet robe swaying on the gentle breezes. The reflections of thousands of shimmering stars radiated in all directions and swirled around him.

Angie exclaimed, "It's Orion! Great to see you!"

"Great to see all of you, " he replied.

"Why are you here?" asked Angie

"Whenever there is an imbalance anywhere, one of my important duties is to investigate. Angie, think back to your outburst, which sent us all scrambling."

With head bent low, Angie gave her remorseful reply, "Yes, I do. I hope everyone totally forgets that incident one day very soon."

Orion continued, "Don't worry. It is no longer a concern to anyone. But this time, we have an imbalance on this new planet. I have been working with Archangel Gersisa, and she has asked me to explain the inner workings of a planet with special emphasis on the Ley Lines."

"Please do explain," requested Andrew, whose love of factual information had piqued his interest.

Orion produced a dark, steaming mass that pulsated in his hands. "Here is a sample of the inner earth. How can I have people, animals, and nature thrive on its surface? Inside we have red hot substances, reservoirs of water larger than oceans, along with all types of gases. Unharnessed volatile energy is ready to explode the energy built up. How can we contain it and make the surface safe?

"First, let's throw a netting over it to hold everything in place. The meshwork is called Ley Lines. They consist of a magnetic field allowing energy to travel everywhere and then return to the heart of the planet.

"In the sample in my hand, you will it pulsating where pressure builds up, and the netting becomes unstable. On planets, a volcano can burst forth from the mountain tops, or an earthquake can split the planet-wide open, releasing the pressure. However, suppose we install some strategically placed pressure release areas. In that case, we can allow the energy to escape."

"What happened this time?" asked Andrew.

"It became obvious that something went wrong, and the delicate balance was disturbed, resulting in an earthquake and volcano release topside. While you restored peace and calm to the occupants, Archangel Gersisa, and Archangel Selaphiel, the Archangel of Prayers, and Archangel Butyalil, the Archangel in charge of the planet's delicate balance, repaired the damage. Fixing the weakness is not enough. If the interplanetary force is too powerful, it needs a means of escape for the future."

Orion stepped back, and Archangel Gersisa stepped forward saying, "The Ley Lines that Orion mentioned are an intricate energy grid formed in straight lines and in perfect alignment. At specific points on the planet's surface, energy centers connect all the Ley Lines and provide a release valve. Visitors from other planets use these centers for guidance and for refueling their craft. They are linked with underground streams and magnetic currents. Where multiple lines converge, reserve centers are installed. Crystals or other naturally occurring elements can amplify the power of the grid.

On Earth, the energy centers include the pyramids, Stonehenge, the Wall of China, and so many more. When Atlantis submerged, the Ley Lines were repositioned to exist above the sunken continent and within the underwater structures."

"So, how will you proceed on Tenalp?" asked Angie.

"The earthquake signaled the need for energy-releasing centers. Legna has organized a work crew to create a pyramid for the first one. Through the use of magnets, they will effortlessly move boulders into place.

"The primitive people will not find any energy centers for multitudes of thousands of years to come. Millions of years into the future, planetary occupants will still wonder about the purpose of pyramids.

Chapter 37 – Energy Center:
Featuring Archangels Selaphiel & Butyalil

"Now, I promised Archangel Michael that I would introduce you to two other Archangels. First, let's welcome Archangel Selaphiel."

A red mist gently moved toward them like fog rolling in. As it got closer, an Archangel emerged with hands crossed over his chest. When he lowered his hands, you could see he held a container of water and two fish. His crimson robe was trimmed in gold, and a gold belt encircled his waist. He was looking downward. As he raised his eyes, he revealed his kind, loving face. A gentle warmth permeated the area leaving hands and feet tingling.

Angie thought, *I will always remember Selaphiel as my red angel.*

"Hello. Yes, Angie, I am one of the red angels. My electromagnetic energy frequency corresponds to the red angel light ray. Do you remember Archangel Uriel? He leads all the red angels. Many of us focus on prayers.

"I have many tasks that justify my presence on Tenalp, especially after the disturbance. I work with countless Archangels, many of whom you have already met. I help rule the movement of the planets and am working with Orion and Gersisa. I work with Phanuel to help preside over exorcisms. Ariana and I work to help protect the children. I even have worked with Archangel Sandalphon bringing forth prayerful music."

"Why haven't we heard about you before, especially when we were working with the other Archangels?" asked Mary.

"There are so many of us. It is best to work with a few at a time to avoid confusion. You don't have to remember which Archangel to call. Send a request to 'Dear Archangels,' and the Archangels will send the one who can best meet your needs. It was so much fun to go on the outings with you and Sandalphon, accompanied by the Irish Jig and fairy harp music tunes. I was right there, but we thought it best that you focus on one Archangel at a time. Sandalphon, with his bobbing and trailing musical notes, was chosen to lead you. Do you understand?"

"Yes, we do!" exclaimed Angie. "It is comforting to know that other Archangels may be helping while just out of sight."

"I want to thank you for calming the community. I am the Archangel of Prayer. It is my task to hear the wishes and fears of the people. You helped relieve the stress, and I helped block out distractions, which allowed the occupants to concentrate on begging for help. They don't understand formal prayer yet."

He became serious as he continued, "Every thought we think, and every word we speak becomes a prayer throughout the universal interconnectedness. Frequently, you have been the answer to someone's prayers, and you didn't even realize it. When the people became afraid and agitated and cried out, they did not realize that they were praying. To answer those prayers, Gersisa jumped into action to find the problem. Christiel spread her calming love over the area. You, in answer to their pleadings, worked with Purlimiek and Fhelyai."

"We had no idea," commented Angie.

"None of us realized this," added Mary.

"Please remember that all requests, whether in a panic state or not and perhaps in thanks, are always heard. You do not have to fold your hands, kneel and close your eyes to pray. We love it when you do because it centers you in prayer and helps you focus. You may call upon me whenever and however you wish. Now that we have met, I will be visible to you. I look forward to seeing you in the future."

They exchanged archangel hugs and watched him depart as his red mist drifted out over the treetops.

Archangel Gersisa once again took her place before them. "Next, let's welcome an angel that is very dear to my heart, Archangel Butyalil, my twin flame. He is in charge of the delicate balance of the planet's place in the cosmos. He can direct his stabilizing energy down through the pyramids and other energy centers back through the Ley Lines. He maintains synchronicity throughout the currents of the universe including all living beings."

A brilliant Archangel with multicolored orbs floating all around him eased its way toward them. His mighty golden wings emitted a blinding white light creating rainbow prisms with the orbs. The light around his head infused the cosmos with the light energy spreading it far and wide and gently showering light over the audience's heads and bodies.

"They are like the waterless mists on the ship. You can't feel them," commented Andrew.

Angie thought, *I'm so glad he is arriving slowly, or we could have been blinded in a flash of light.*

He held a green cylindrical object. Beneath its translucent surface, you could make out brightly shining gold and white lines as he rotated the object in his hand.

"Greetings. I am Archangel Butyalil, and I am honored to meet you and to thank you for all your efforts in calming the people. At the same time, Gersisa and I worked on the inner planet and Ley Lines. I am happy to report that all is well and as it should be. Under my guidance, Legna will work on pyramidal energy centers to help maintain balance. I believe you have amassed an enormous amount of knowledge over the past couple of days. You have received first-hand knowledge that we didn't expect. I must go but first, archangels' hugs for all."

As they hugged him, they looked closely at the orb in his hands. And then he was gone.

"Archangel Gersisa. Is the green round object he held in his hand a model of Tenalp?" asked Angie.

"Yes, my child. How very observant of you. The white and gold markings within the ball symbolize the Ley Lines."

"That reminds me of the song, "He Has the Whole World in his Hands," remarked Angie.

"Excellent analogy. I thoroughly enjoyed my time with you and Purlimiek. Yes, I was there. I work very closely with nature. It is a necessary part of achieving balance. It is time for you to return to the craft and get some much-needed rest and relaxation. More hugs before you go?"

They welcomed the extra hugs and then reached for Legna. They were back on the craft smiling because of the good news of Tenalp. Their exhausted minds were brimming with new information. After a snack, they turned in for the night.

Part IV
Until We Meet Again

Chapter 38 – Archangel Council:
Featuring 30 Archangels

A note to the readers: For more information on the archangels and their specialties, refer to the Appendix.

The following day their favorite wind chime alarm gently lulled them from their sound sleep.

Angie asked out loud, to no one in particular, "What could possibly be next?"

"I have no idea," replied Andrew. "We have learned so much, and the planet seems to be progressing smoothly. Maybe it is time for a new mission? Maybe we are done, and it's time to go back home?"

They dressed in silent thought and then found Mary and Matthew in the Nutrition area. They stood around the table, helping themselves to some of their favorite breakfast goodies while they quizzed each other on what the future had in store for them. Legna stopped by and requested that they come to the Astral Room as soon as they finished.

In-depth conversations heightened, and between mouthfuls, the group continued to ponder their future. "It can't be anything catastrophic, or they would have summoned us with urgency," stated Andrew.

Curiosity propelled them into high gear as they rushed to the Astral Room. Overspilling into the hallway was a twinkling of stars that they had come to recognize immediately. They ran in and straight into Orion's archangel hug.

Gently interrupting the love fest, Archangel Michael asked them to please take their seats. There was no gazebo on this day. Inquisitiveness continued to squelch their concentration with thoughts of uncertainty. *Michael has arrived and seems happy, so there is no cause for concern*, thought Angie

"Welcome everyone," greeted Archangel Michael. "Orion and I are here to extend a special invitation to you from the Archangels. You are guests of honor at a special council. Return to your rooms to put on your finery and then gather here. We don't want to keep the council waiting, so we will be departing soon. Please return quickly."

Angie was bursting with questions, but she knew that the sooner they got ready, the quicker she would get her answers. And she was right. In record time, they had assembled and transported to a private meeting room in the School of Wisdom. They took their places on stage with Michael and Orion at their sides.

"Before we get started, we have another Guest of Honor to welcome. Legna. As you are aware, Legna, with the assistance of his crew, has been invaluable, and we want to express our sincere appreciation to all of them."

Legna received a multitude of individual thanks and praise. Michael continued. "There are 15 Archangels with whom you worked when you rescued the loving souls. And there are 15 Archangels with whom you had not worked with until Tenalp. Let us welcome the council of these 30 archangels.

With exquisite majesty, the first 15 glided into the room.

Ariel entered and her pretty pale pink intermingled with the dark pink of Jophiel accompanied by the sound of their favorite wind chimes.

The pale green of Chamuel joined with Raphael's healing green light accentuated by the cooper of Gabriel.

The twinkling bright, white of Azrael contrasted with the dark purple of Jeremiel and was a perfect backdrop for Raguel's pale blue and Zadkiel's deep indigo-blue glittering mist.

Uriel's yellow sunbeams highlighted the room, overlayed by Raziel's rainbow colors and alternating with Haniel's pale blue moonbeams.

Metatron's Merkabah cube, in shades of pink and green, spun in all directions while Sandalphon's tropical turquoise ocean flooded the room with musical notes.

When the last of the original fourteen Archangels entered, Michael went up to join the others in his royal blue and gold colors.

The Archangels interacted joyfully with each other. Their colorful energies were bobbing and weaving like kites swirling on a windy day. Love, peace, calm, and appreciation filled the vibrations in the room.

The colors of these 15 Archangels whom Angie, Andrew, Mary, and Matthew, knew so well and loved beyond imagination, was a gorgeous sight to behold. They could not speak or move for what seems like ages, mesmerized by the sights and sounds.

Michael returned to his place on the podium and announced, "Archangels, thank you for the lovely display. Please move to the perimeter. I will invite 15 more Archangels to join us. An opening appeared, and Orion, surrounded by millions of stairs, rose to fill the space with his light and love.

Archangel Michael returned to his place behind the podium. "Thank you, Orion, and thank you to this council of 15 Archangels. Let us invite 14 more Archangels, who had recently worked with our special guests. Please join Orion and delight us with your colorful light show."

Mariel's brushstrokes of magenta accented Manakel's crystal-clear blue ocean, and both accentuated the blue of Ariana. Barachiel's lush green robe with lightning bolts pierced the sky while his rose petals drifted to the floor.

Nathaniel's bright red with streaks of orange flames complimented the powdery blue of his twin flame, Ariana. Phanuel's calm pale blue, with his doves of peace, flew through the room with no sign of his fiery angry red side on this loving day.

Arariel, with her rainy mist, joined Gadiel with his shades of brilliant yellow intermittently blending with his shades of green.

Gersisa's flawless steel gray changed to a sparkly silver and then back again. Prisms radiated in all directions. Butyalil was by her side, with multicolored orbs floating all around him. Mighty golden wings emitted a blinding white light creating rainbow prisms with the orbs. He held a green cylindrical object.

Christiel, emitting a golden, calming mist, sent forth peace and love with Purlimiek's pale soft blue-green light. Fhelyai's sunny yellow sunlight rays bounced from his aura, bathing the area in the warmth of the sun while Selaphiel's crimson robe and red mist rolled in.

The second group of Archangels' unique colors swirled together in a synchronized dance, enchanting all with a breathtaking performance.

Archangel Michael said, "I invite all the Archangels to join together as we say thank you to Angie, Andrew, Mary, Matthew, and Legna for their assistance on the mission to colonize Tenalp.

The colonists are doing well and have once again found love in their hearts.

The room came alive beyond imagination. It was truly magical. The foursome watched in awe, recognizing different Archangels and sending greetings up to them.

"Thank you one and all. Please return to your places," instructed Michael. "Our mission has been completed. Many of you will continue to watch over the planet and offer suggestions for new experiences. However, it is time for us to let Angie, Andrew, Mary, Matthew, and Legna return to their homeworld to spend time with their families. As you leave the room, please stop by and offer an archangel hug of thanks to our special guests."

Angie was ecstatic at the thought of receiving archangel hugs, one after another, to a total count of 30.

Soon, only Michael remained and announced, "We have another exciting journey planned. I will meet you in the Astral Room tomorrow morning, and we will depart from there. Legna, please take our special guests back to the aircraft where they can bask in the recollections of this momentous day. I will see you all tomorrow, including Legna, who will join us on our next surprise outing.

Chapter 39 – Glistening

They had difficulty falling asleep with the surreal images of the Archangel Council swirling through the pages of their minds. Intermittent musings floated by as they wondered where tomorrow would take them. Exhaustion finally overtook them, and they were swept up into colorful dreams until the twinkling of wind chimes brought them back to reality.

After a hurried breakfast, the foursome made their way to the Astral Room, where they found Michael and Legna deep in discussions.

"Good morning, and I hope you enjoyed yesterday," commented Michael.

"Yes, we did!" came a chorus that echoed around the room.

"Thank you so much," added Angie, with her friends nodding in agreement. "It was beautiful, and we loved seeing old and new friends. It was such a delightful surprise, and the memories will stay with us forever. So many archangel hugs to comfort us no matter what the future brings. Speaking of the future, do we have more work to do on Tenalp? Will we be going home soon?"

"My dear sweet Angie, who fills the atmosphere with her multitude of questions, you will have to trust us. It will be more enjoyable that way. Over the next couple of days, we have some outings planned. Our destinations will remain a secret. Please don't smother us with questions. Just sit back and enjoy the journey and the surprises that will unfold before you," instructed Michael. "Legna will be your tour guide. I'll join you during the last leg of this multifaceted journey. Enjoy the suspense and surprises."

To avoid tempting Angie to plead for details, he was gone. Angie could hardly contain herself and appeared to be ready to burst. Andrew reached out and took her hand to help calm and center her. Mary remained quiet and poised. While she didn't like surprises, she loved everything they had done so far. As long as nothing was scary, she would be patient. Matthew knew he could wait but wondered if there would be any delectable cuisine.

Legna explained that they would travel in the shuttlecraft for the first leg of their journey and escorted them to the shuttle bay. They quickly settled into their chairs and were underway. The ship skimmed the ocean blue through the sparkling sunlight of millions of diamonds reflecting off the calm waters.

I know where we are going, pondered Angie, while the others silently agreed. Andrew squeezed her hand, reminding her not to speak. Questions flooded their minds as they shared their silent thoughts.

As soon as Belau, with its patchwork of small islands, came into view, they collectively knew where they were going. The names *Bubble Palace and Hcar* escaped from Angie's mind and into the cockpit.

Legna's stern look silenced the excited foursome. They saw some Belauns around the many waterfalls peeking through the expansive treetops. Others were out on their canoes. They peered intently, looking for the father and sons they had seen before but no such any luck.

"Remember that we are cloaked, and they cannot see us," remarked Legna.

Their craft left the small islands behind as they hastened forward, skimming the wave tops through their prisms of sparking light. In the distance, they saw the familiar smooth, waveless patch on the ocean surface.

Legna announced, "We are here!" The craft gently sliced through the water, heading downward, leaving the diamond sparkles behind replaced by prisms of bright turquoise.

They gently bumped the lush kelp towers initiating a swaying dance before them. Schools of tropical fish darted through and illuminated the undergrowth. *Beautiful* escaped from the contemplations of their minds. All of a sudden, there it was, the enormous bubble residences atop the lush, vibrant coral reef. They were all thrilled and anxious beyond belief, knowing they would soon see their friends. Effortlessly, they came to rest on the landing pad and entered through the glass door. Water drained from the enclosure, and they rushed to meet their friends.

"Hcar! Zcar! Hello! It is so great to see you," exclaimed Angie.

"Welcome back to Eungem," greeted Hcar and Zcar in unison. Their young children rushed forward to exchange hugs. Enthusiastically, the young ones practically dragged their guests to their home. Legna promised to meet them after he took care of some business.

Overwhelmed by the beauty of the tropical aquarium that surrounded them, Angie stated, "Your home is as beautiful as ever, and we are so grateful to be here with all of you. Michael and Legna would not tell us we were going. What an awesome surprise!"

"Please sit and enjoy," suggested Zcar. "I've prepared some salad for our lunch. I'll leave you so I can prepare the table."

"Can we help?" asked Mary

"No, thank you. Please enjoy the beauty which we are fortunate to experience every day. Our sons will point out some reef visitors and dwellers for you."

Two enthusiastic young ones were animated as they pointed out every treasure they could find. The delighted guests were a willingly captive audience.

Zcar announced, "Food is ready. Please take a seat."

The chairs were all positioned on one side of the table for everyone's viewing enjoyment. Their dining was occasionally interrupted by someone pointing out a newfound discovery.

When they finished their meal, Mary said, "Thank you. The meal was delicious, and the coral reef is a wonderous delight."

"You are very welcome," replied Czar. "It has been a pleasure having you. We don't get many visitors, and you have become special guests to us. Let's retire to our living area. We would love to hear what you have been up to since our last visit."

Hcar led the way to comfortable seats again arranged for optimal viewing. While witnessing the spectacular mesmerizing show and the interruptions of the children when a unique visitor came into view, they relayed their experiences at Tenalp. They spoke of the advent of fire and the warming of the crude caves and their food. They explained the damming of the small stream, creating bathing and washing areas along with playful pools for fun. They relayed the story of the earthquake and how the natural plants helped calm the occupants. The children became spellbound in-between asking an outpouring of questions, reminding Angie of herself.

Legna returned and announced, "It is time to go. The plans for this day are not complete. We have another destination and must be on our way."

The festive gathering turned somber as their visit came to an end. They exchanged mutual thanks and gratitude. There were no 'Goodbyes.' Instead, they said, "until we meet again," complete with hugs, smiles, and promises of virtual visits on the computers.

Legna circled the bubble homes, and they were delighted to find Hcar and his family watching for them. With a last farewell wave, they were on their way back to the mothercraft in silence as the recollections of their visit were added to their treasured memories.

Chapter 40 – Diamonds

Once back on board, they settled into their seats on the observation deck.

"Thank you so much for that wonderful surprise. We love that underwater community, and we love Hcar's family. Thank you," Angie joyfully and appreciatively commented and then meekly asked, "Can you tell us where we are going next?"

"No," Legna responded. "However, you will know soon enough."

They enjoyed the ride past planets and zillions of stars, asteroids, and meteorites.

"Is that Orion?" asked Andrew. If it was, Orion did not stay still long enough to let his presence be known.

Legna increased to warp speed, and they enjoyed the tunnel of light that brought them closer to their destination. They thought they were going to Tenalp but were overjoyed to see Legna's barren planet surface and thrilled and surprised with this secret destination

With engines turned off, they quietly descended to the parking area. They looked up in time to see the landing pad rise to the ceiling, hiding them from inquiring passersby.

Legna instructed, "My family is waiting for you in the garden area. Enjoy gathering some food for our meal. Here are your visors. Remember to put them on when you enter the living area."

"You don't have to remind me," stated Angie, almost reliving the glare and pain she had suffered during the last visit when she tried to peak from under the visor.

They excitedly boarded the transporter and selected the ideal viewing seats. In silence, they watched the enormous farmlands stretch out before them. The crystal planting beds sparkled and twinkled against the backdrop of the greenery mixed with the bright colors of the fruits and vegetables.

"There they are!" exclaimed Angie. Waiting for them were Legna's wife, Rednow, holding onto their daughter, Ria's hand, with their sons, Nos and Yob, by her sides.

When the transporter halted, the guests quickly disembarked, running into their hosts' waiting arms. Aliens were usually so proper, but Angie and her friends didn't care. Joy overwhelmed them at the realization that they were back at Nerrab, so they had to express their happiness in the human form of hugging. Ria, who had been shy and clung to her Mom on the former visit, ran right into Angie's embrace, and soon everyone was hugging while sharing warm, welcoming smiles.

"It is so good to be back," stated Mary.

"Oh yes, it is," agreed Angie.

"I hope we have time to share a meal," commented Matthew.

"Of course," stated Rednow. "Let's gather some food together."

Nos and Yob gathered food at Rednow's direction, and soon the basket was overflowing with salad makings including nuts, seeds, and fruits as well as greens, tomatoes, carrots, celery, cucumbers, and so much more.

"Nos and Yob! Take Ria with you and gather and plant the replacements. Don't forget to start some new seedlings," instructed Rednow.

"We can help too!" offered the guests.

"Thank you. I appreciate your assistance. I'll return to our home and prepare the salads. Don't forget to wear your visors," warned Rednow.

"It will be fun. We enjoy your children," confirmed Mary.

When they finished planting, the children led their visitors to the archway. The blinding light spilling out of the entryway reminded the guests to put their visors on. The brightness of the crystals within inflicts excruciating pain on human eyes. Legna's people are born with a protective eye covering.

With see-through visors securely in place, they entered the living communities. A familiar sight, once again, had them in awe. crystal waterfall was a sight to behold. Beyond the waterfall was the massive lake with calm ripples that kissed the diamond banks of the shoreline. They looked up toward the blue crystal sky with yellow crystal accents that mimicked the sun and provided sunlight.

"Everything is as beautiful as I remember it!" rejoiced Angie.

"Yes, it is, and I'm so glad Legna has brought us back here," remarked Mary.

"Let's get back to their residence so we can enjoy a meal," suggested Matthew.

The anxious young ones, who had seen enough of their familiar sight, directed the group toward the crystal, green hallways leading to the homes.

The children pulled them right into the Saffire blue living quarters with the highly polished flat floors and walls adorned with rounded crystal half-spheres. Rednow had the table set and was just bringing out the salads. Legna was already there waiting for them.

"Please let us eat and then let us talk and explain to the inquiring minds about your adventures on Tenalp," suggested Legna.

"The food is delicious, and the company is delightful!" exclaimed Angie. "We thought we were going to Tenalp when we saw your planet. This surprise is absolutely marvelous and a very much appreciated surprise."

Mary and Angie helped Rednow clear the table and refill the water glasses. Nos and Yob were anxious to hear about their adventures and pleaded, "Please tell us all about everything you have been doing with our Dad."

Ria climbed up onto Angie's lap bring a smile to her face and a nod from Rednow. For the second time that day, the foursome explained how lightning split an old tree trunk into two, and the dried leaves help set it on fire. Andrew explained how a strong man pulled one of the burning logs into the dark, damp cave, which turned bright and warm.

Then they explained how they secretly dammed a stream creating ponds for washing and swimming.

"It is hard to believe how anyone could live without clean water," remarked Yob.

"Yes, and you should have seen their dirty faces and clothes. They were eating on dirty plates too," explained Mary.

Andrew provided details of the earthquake and the people who kept running in and out of their cave. He spoke of the calming mist that settled over the area thanks to the Archangels. Together, they took turns explaining how they collected Sandalwood, Patchouli, Chamomile, and Frankincense and how they secretly brought them to the outdoor fire at night.

"And we had a picnic in a beautiful field, complete with picnic baskets," added Matthew.

Mary said, "And we witnessed butterflies that covered entire trees and created a wonderous site when they took flight only to return and cover the tree again with their gorgeous wings."

They talked for hours, providing specific details and answering a myriad of questions. All too soon, Legna said it was time to go.

"No! Please let them stay longer!" the children implored.

"I'm sorry, but we must depart to keep to our schedule. This day has been very long and emotional. Our guests must get some rest to prepare for tomorrow's secret surprise. Archangel Michael will be waiting for us first thing tomorrow morning."

"We will visit over the computers," suggested Andrew. Everyone promised to stay in touch while hugs and smiles filled the room. Once again, they avoided saying 'goodbye,' but instead, they said 'until we meet again.'

They were quiet as they rode on the transporter and boarded the spacecraft. More memories filled the pages of their minds. They were exhausted from two momentous visits in this one day.

When they got back on board the spacecraft, Legna said, "Please sleep while my crew guides us to our next destination. It is another surprise, so no questions. I'll awaken you with your favorite wind chimes. We will meet in the Astral Room after you have breakfast. Goodnight."

Chapter 41 – We Did It

The sound of wind chimes interrupted their dreams of underwater coral reefs and crystal palaces.

"I wonder where they plan to take us today?" asked Angie, stretching and anxious to welcome a new day.

"Let's get going, and we will soon find out," suggested Andrew.

They joined Mary and Matthew in the Nutrition Area. Discussions, reflecting where they had been, along with whispered musings of where they might be going, accompanied the sounds around the breakfast table.

Angie whispered, "I wonder if we will be going to the Meet-and Greet-Area next,"

"Sounds great to me!" acknowledged Andrew, fondly reflecting on past visits of spending quality time with Angie.

"Let's finish up and get going so we can find out if they will give us any hints before we get there," suggested Mary.

Michael and Legna were waiting in the Astral Room.

"Thank you so very much for taking us back to Eungem and Nerrab and the wonderful visits with our newfound special friends. We didn't expect either of those surprises and are so grateful," announced Angie, with the others expressing their appreciation.

"It is time to get going, and no, don't ask where. It will remain a surprise, so you won't know where we are going until we arrive. I'll meet you there. See you soon," stated Michael before he departed.

They relocated to the observation deck, and once settled in their seats, Legna accelerated to warp speed. They watched the light show tunnel while they continued to wonder what they would see once the craft returned to cruising speed, and when it did, "Tenalp!" cried out Angie. "That is a surprise! Do we have more work to do?"

"We will take the shuttle down to Mount Overlook, where we will meet with Archangel Michael, who will fill you in on the details."

As the shuttle approached Mount Overlook, they observed their favorite traveling gazebo decorated with all the flowers that had graced and decorated it during the different visits from the Archangels. There were the Peace Lilly's and the bobbing faces of the Pansies. There were night-blooming Moonflowers, magenta pink Pansies, and Water Lilies with red rose petals scattered about the floor. The various scents mingled and tickled their noses

Michael welcomed them and advised, "Today is your last visit to Tenalp. There are no tasks to complete. You are here to observe the occupants and witness once more all of the pioneering accomplishments you helped make possible.

It was a lovely day with a Magenta sunrise and rainbows in the distance. They all knew that all the archangels would make this day unbelievably magical to add to the memory scrapbook of this trip.

"The archangels will not be visible to you this day. They said their farewells at the Ceremony. However, they are all working behind the scenes, and yes, to make sure this day a wondrous memory to take with you.

They boarded a cloaked smaller spacecraft which allowed them to take a closer look at the community. The transport skimmed over the treetops and landed in the clearing in front of the empty cave.

They witnessed the fire within casting shadows of flames up the walls. The outside fire was still burning. The residents added another dried log next to the original.

"They understand how to get more fire!" exclaimed Angie. "That is wonderful! I wonder if we will recognize the gigantic male with muscles like an ox who dragged the first log into the cave?"

"And look!" exclaimed Andrew. They have a stack of Sandalwood and see the Patchouli and Frankincense around the fire."

"And, I can see Chamomile that they must be using in tea," Mary pointed out.

"Look there," Matthew said, pointing toward a thriving garden. "They are becoming very resourceful."

"I wonder if we will recognize the walk-in with the physical handicap that we met on the Astral Plane, although it will be hard to know if they have changed places yet," stated Mary.

"Let's take a ride around and see what else we can see," suggested Legna.

They traveled toward the steam, which now had many offshoots and ponds.

"It is amazing how they realized they could direct and dam the waters to their added benefit. And to think we started them in this direction," commented Angie. "And, Oh look! There is Brook. She is intelligent, and I'm sure the angels give her thoughts that she puts into good use."

"I can see Sky and Stormy over there," pointed out Mary. "They are holding hands out in the open. I wonder if there will be a baby in their future."

"There certainly will be," stated Angie. "Look more closely. Sky is pregnant!"

"Everyone looks so much cleaner and happier," observed Mary. "And we helped do this! I sense love in the air everywhere."

"I hope the negative souls do not incarnate here anytime soon," commented Angie.

"Don't worry about that," cautioned Andrew. "We all feel confident the Archangels will make sure they don't come here before they are ready."

As Legna motored the craft away from the people, they found their picnic spot. Legna set down in an isolated area where they found picnic baskets spread out on a blanket.

"Enjoy your lunch and give a whistle to watch the butterfly displays again," suggested Legna.

"Will you join us?" invited Mary.

"No, thank you. I have some business to attend to. I'll be here in the craft until you have finished your picnic."

They found containers of their favorite salads, which they thoroughly enjoyed in this magical setting. Andrew gave a whistle or two and the butterflies complied with delightful performances for their viewing delight.

Not wanting to leave but not wanting to keep Legna waiting, they reluctantly returned to the craft.

"There is one more place, a proud accomplishment, that I would like to show you. Sit back, and I'll let you know when and where to look," instructed Legna. It wasn't long before he instructed, "Look to your right!"

"Wow! A pyramid!" announced Andrew.

Towering high into the atmosphere was a pyramid just like the ones they were familiar with on Earth I and Earth II.

Legna explained. "A team of my people has been hard at work moving the stones into place. It is now fully operational as an energy release center. The people that live in this area of Tenalp should never experience another earthquake. All we have left to do is plant greenery on all sides to keep it hidden from view. It will look like a mountain, and no one will be the wiser.

"That is an amazing fete," remarked Andrew. "I am very impressed."

"And we thank you because we never want these people to experience the fright of another earthquake," stated Mary.

They returned to the gazebo where Michael waited for them.

"I hope you weren't waiting long," stated Angie.

"No, I never have to wait. I always arrive at exactly the correct time," explained Michael.

"I understand," stated Angie with a giggle. "We all thoroughly enjoyed seeing the community and how they have taken the knowledge we imparted to them and have moved forward. Will we ever see these people again?"

"There is a good possibility," stated Michael. "People will come and go while the planet continues to advance, but the foundation has been set and will remain for all time. When the time comes for the addition of new communities, there will be more work to do."

"We look forward to helping where and whenever we can," confirmed Andrew.

"This is goodbye for now," continued Michael. "We will always be nearby and available whenever you need us or just want to say hello. Before you return to Earth II, Legna will take you to the Meet-and-Greet Area. Best wishes to you. Enjoy your extended family and each other. Share stories of your adventures."

Michael gave departing archangel hugs and was gone. The group held hands with Legna and whisked off to the spacecraft with satisfying accomplishing visions of Tenalp in their minds.

Chapter 42 – Reunion

After a good night's sleep, they revisited the Meet-and-Greet area, where they nuzzled with their favorite unicorns.

A babbling brook only a foot deep and about ten feet wide ran through the field. It always reminded Angie of her beloved Jenny Jump State Park. Their favorite mystical, magical unicorns were frolicking in the water's edge. They held a special place in the hearts of Angie, Andrew, Mary, and Matthew because they were the first unicorns they had seen in a very long time. Poachers had killed them for their horns to the point of extinction on Earth I. Now, they enjoyed their safe sanctuary on Earth II.

They heard a commotion and turned to see Dalmatians romping over to greet them. Bosco, Patches, and Junior—Angie, and Andrew's childhood pets—were so happy their bodies shook. Sinbad, Andrew's childhood lab, was there too. Angie and Andrew's pet birds, canaries, parakeets, cockatiels, and parrot, waited for Angie to stretch out her arms so they could settle down. Tweeting, trilling, and some parrot dialogue filled the air. Mary and Matthew were showered with love by some of their childhood pets. Unconditional love abounded.

Andrew reminded them, "Archangel Michael invited our deceased loved ones to join us for this visit. We should be going."

Reluctantly but agreeably, they let the birds take flight, shooed the dogs away, and made their way to the banquet hall.

Angie's parents were tending to their gardens, and Andrew's parents were there doing some gardening as well. On the way, Angie saw her dad admiring roses in exquisite colors, including some shades of red, pink, and yellow. Their petals looked like velvet. He seemed so content in his rose garden.

Then she noticed her mother-in-law surrounded by her favorite pale-violet lilacs. The hydrangea bushes were teeming with multicolored blooms the size of dinner plates that bounced around like pom-poms. An entire fence was full of every color of morning glory imaginable. Her mother-in-law looked so happy among her favorite flowers.

Canna lilies, tiger lilies, caladiums, gladiolas, geraniums, marigolds, zinnias, alyssum, snapdragons, and more were exquisitely displayed and adorned in their colorful dress. She saw her mom admiring them and the hanging baskets overflowing with gorgeous blooms. The color palette was spectacular. These were all her mom's favorites, and she looked so happy tending to them. Amid the delightful fragrances of all the flowers, Angie caught a whiff of her mom's favorite perfume.

The gardeners waved their greetings and after hugs and kisses, joined them, hand-in-hand, to complete their walk to the Banquet Hall.

Their parents, best friends, aunts, uncles, cousins, and grandparents were everywhere. They didn't have to relate any stories of where they had been or what they were up to because everyone already knew. Instead, they shared memories of weddings, births, fun outings, and other special occasions they had enjoyed together. It was a glorious visit, and when they finished enjoying their appetizers, they took their places at the table for a favorite meal of their choosing. Angie, Andrew, Mary, and Matthew sat at the head of the table as the honored guests at their farewell party.

Andrew stood up and offered a toast, "Thank you all for being with us this day. It means so much. Recently, we have been here many times without you because those visits were to rejuvenate us for our next task. Today we rest, celebrate, and enjoy this wonderful company before our return home. We will be back, so for now, I toast with the words, 'Until we meet again!'"

Glasses tinkled, and acknowledgments resounded. A conversational din filled the room to be silenced when personally selected delectable dessert courses appeared before them.

At nightfall, before the moon had fully risen in the sky, their guests left them with the departing words, 'Until we meet again.' They returned to their chalets once again, where the moonlight sprinkled its path on the water. Angie and Andrew swung on their porch swing. Mary and Matthew were doing the same on the porch of their separate chalet. They relaxed while more splendid memories of the reunion filled flooded their minds.

When they ventured inside, they found the fireplace ablaze and settled into the comfy floor pillows to gaze at the flames that helped them drift off to sleep. It was a deep sleep from the exhaustion of the past couple of days shrouded with memory-type dreams of their farewell visits.

Wind chimes awoke them. The fire had died down, and the sun was rising, chasing the moon out of the sky. The soul mates hugged and made their way to the banquet hall, where they found Matthew and Mary enjoying their breakfast. The conversation was at a minimum while they ate. Once they leaned back in their chairs, they started to reminisce, once again, where they had been and whom they had seen. The conversations went on for a very long time before restlessness set in, and they decided to visit their favorite unicorns for one final farewell visit.

Chapter 43 – Home at Last

The ride back home seemed to take forever, wrapped up in their eagerness to see their family. They wiled away the hours playing games and contacting Legna's and Hcar's families with thanks for everything, including the cherished memories for their delightful visits. They enjoyed meals, reminisced with the crew, and even found time to visit the molecular room.

The next morning, Legna joined them for breakfast in the Community Room. Words of appreciation choked up through tearful goodbyes. Angie took Legna aside to thank him specifically for the special assistance he had given her with her concern over the non-loving souls. Emotions ran high between wanting to get home and not wanting to leave Legna and his fantastic crew. They all promised to keep in touch, and Legna agreed to let them know when he was at the airstrip so they could come visit.

Legna sent word ahead of their arrival time, so a great crowd was there to greet them when they touched down. "Welcome home" banners and cheers greeted them when Angie, Andrew, Mary, and Matthew descended from the craft.

"It is so great to be back home!" exclaimed Angie.

"Yes, but I do miss everyone and every place we visited on this last trip," agreed Mary.

"The food was awesome, but I am looking forward to some of Wendy's home-cooked meals," added Matthew.

"I am so thankful that Legna and Archangel Michael took us on some surprise farewell visits," confirmed Andrew, to echoes of 'us too.'

Like a parade, they all marched to the homestead, passing the unicorns along the way. Wendy had prepared a feast for all to enjoy, and that night, they sat around and talked before exhaustion took its toll. Their adventure had been long and tedious but was well worth it, especially with this homecoming.

The next morning, the aroma from the kitchen was mesmerizing. Angie, Andrew, Mary, and Matthew followed their noses to the kitchen table where family members were already partaking in the delicacies laid out and enticing them. When they all had their fill, they settled down on the porch, with coffees in hand. The conversation turned to making plans of all they wanted to do and see now that they were back home. Although they had plenty of time, or so they thought, they could not contain their excitement to visit their two-legged, four-legged, and even no-legged friends, the trees. They mapped out a plan with Wendy's help, including unicorns, fairies, leprechauns, and the tree people. Their top priority was a celebration with family, friends and a delicious spread of their favorite foods to make up for all the holidays they had missed.

Angie added, "I know we missed the Christmas decorations, so I'd love to see photos."

It was February in Florida, and Mary complimented Wendy. "You have the home decorated with hearts and flowers perfect for our return, but you didn't even know we were coming."

Wendy replied, "This is the month of love and a perfect time for your return. Get freshened up, and let's meet back here in an hour. I'll have some heart-shaped sugar cookies and some hot chocolate ready for a mid-morning snack. I'll grab the Christmas photos too."

They met as planned and poured through the photos narrated by Wendy, who emphasized the happy memories of the holidays, including inviting the fairies in for a River Dance with music compliments of Sandalphon. The sugar cookies and hot chocolate added to the festive remembrances.

"Now it is time for you to tell us all about your trip," suggested Wendy.

"We still have so much to tell, but first, we would like to visit the unicorns," advised Mary.

Matthew chimed in, "how about we meet on the porch after lunch? Invite all the available family members."

"Sounds wonderful. I'll put out some extra chairs and cushions. How about some chocolate chip cookies this afternoon?" offered Wendy.

"Perfect," came the chorus from Angie, Andrew, Mary, and Matthew. "See you later."

The foursome joined hands and skipped down the lane. Without speaking a word of their ultimate destination, they knew they would end up at the gazebo for lunch, and there were no complaints.

When the unicorns spotted them, they galloped over to the fence and nuzzled their friends that they had missed for such an impossibly long time. It was a mutual affection party that continued until Matthew announced that it was lunchtime and time to continue to the gazebo. After a few more hugs with their unicorn friends, they were on their way.

The gazebo looked beautiful and so inviting. Matthew served them while the others spoke of the unicorns and wanting to see the fairies that night. The pizza was delicious, and with full stomachs, they were tired and lazily walked back.

As they made their way, they heard a din which grew louder and louder the closer they got to their home. Rounding the corner, they found the porch full of anxious family members. There were four empty chairs strategically positioned in the middle. The excitement grew louder when the audience spotted their special guests.

Angie had so much she wanted to tell them and started as soon as they were all seated. "We have been working with different archangels, helping teach a new community their fundamental needs, such as introducing them to fire and water. It was so gratifying to see how happy they were when firelight lit their caves and warmed them up."

Mary added, "I don't think I could live a primitive lifestyle. I love the comforts of home too much."

"You could if you had to and didn't know about the comforts you were missing," countered Andrew.

Andrew took over the conversation. "One of the archangels guided lightning to split an old tree. He felled it, and flames from the dead leaves helped teach the occupants the existence of fire. We were thrilled to witness this major milestone. Finger puppets, warm sleeping quarters, cooked food, and so much more opened their eyes to infinite possibilities."

"We helped dam up a stream so they could wash and bathe. It was joyous to see the kids playing in the water. Clean faces became the norm," added Mary.

"When are we going to tell them?" asked Andrew.

"Tell us what? When you have to leave?" How many days before you are gone again?" asked Wendy.

Angie, with a teasing look in her eyes, said, "I have a very important announcement. We have finished our mission. We can stay here for a very long time. If invited on a future mission, we will be ready, but, for now, we have no plans at all."

Squeals of delight filled the air. "Are you serious?" Wendy said.

"We sure are the foursome sang out in unison."

For hours, they spoke of the underwater community but were careful not to mention Legna's diamond homeland. The audience was spellbound when they explained about the scary ground-shaking earthquakes and how the calming mist and soothing plants helped return peace to the community. They briefly spoke of the Ley Lines and soon turned their conversation to the suddenly appearing and then vanishing gazebo. They described the 15 new archangels in great detail, from their gowns to all the accessories, including stars, orbs, sparkles, including the items they held in their hands.

They told them about their home away from home. They mentioned the mattresses that swallowed you up and the storage method reducing them to a flattened size. They explained about the Nutrition Area and the Hydroponic Growing Center. They made plans to grow some herbs. Angie explained about the wall in Legna's office that only opened for him. Andrew, Mary, and Matthew didn't even know about that and were very interested to learn more. They explained the Cleansing Rooms with the waterless mist.

They lost track of time until the sun started to set, casting shadows on the lawn that appeared to elongate the audience.

"It is a good night to serve leftovers if anyone wants to eat. I'll spread out a buffet," invited Wendy.

"I'll help," informed Mary, with Angie agreeing to help too.

Some went home while others made their way into the kitchen. After everyone had eaten and cleaned up, the girls excused themselves and found the guys nodding off in their comfy chairs.

"Let's get some sleep," Angie gently announced so as not to startle the guys. "A visit to the backyard fairyland will have to wait until another night. We have a big day tomorrow. Come. Off to bed."

The following day, after a good night's sleep, the delightful smells of breakfast woke up the sleepyheads. After freshening up, they headed toward the kitchen and found their places at the table. Wendy had planned a dinner party for that evening, and Angie and Mary were anxious to help. The guys helped William with some of his chores. They skipped lunch which was no problem because the water supply gave them all the nutrients their bodies needed. They didn't need to eat, but they loved the variety of tastes and smells. After all they ate since their return, missing a meal wouldn't hurt at all.

The dinner party full of family and delicious food was a memorable event. Dishes made their way around the table, and silverware clanged while conversation and laughter filled the air.

As darkness fell and they had their fill, they helped with the dishes and cleaning the kitchen. The guys got the flashlights, and Wendy led them to the backyard. It looked better than ever with Wendy's addition of more flowers, plants, and tiki torches. Wendy stopped the procession to light their way. Fairy shadows loomed around the yard. Sunny rushed over to greet them. Soon fairies were dancing around all their shoulders. They danced for hours with their friends. It was another exhausting day, and the foursome craved sleep. So many changes during their adventure, and now the changes at home, made for an early bedtime.

The next day, Angie found a free moment to wander down to the beach where she sat and let the tranquil lapping of the shore take her down memory lane. So many Archangels. So many new and wondrous adventures. Despite her worry about the non-loving souls, she loved every minute of the trip. Her mind drifted to their surprise picnic with Fhelyai and collecting the calming Sandalwood, Frankincense, and Chamomile. Images of the butterflies and the 'Hey yo' cries of the Koel birds filled her mind. Soon she found herself in the underwater aquarium where Hcar and his family lived.

In the background, she heard her name. At first, she thought it was Hcar, but as the voice became more apparent, she realized it was Andrew.

"Wendy. Wendy. Wake up, my love," whispered Andrew. She stood up, and Andrew enfolded her into his sweet embrace. He continued to whisper in her ear, "Welcome home, Angie. I love you and loved our adventure. But it is so good to be back home and to be able to relax and enjoy our lovely assortment of memories."

With barely a word, they walked, hand in hand back home. After a day or two of relaxing, much of talking, explaining, baking, eating, and so much more, they were ready to party with the leprechauns.

"Perhaps as early as tomorrow, we can do a day trip to the leprechauns, fairies, and Tree People. I'll reach out to Sandalphon and Ariel and see if they can make the arrangements and accompany us once again," offered Angie.

Chapter 44 – Merriment

Bright and early, they woke to sounds from their favorite songs. A medley of verses intrigued their minds into waking. Once it dawned on them what they were hearing, they rushed to the front porch. The sounds of music filled the air. Sandalphon greeted them with his entourage of musical notes, keeping time. His tropical attire was refreshing.

Ariel said, "Hello," and her voice blended in with the music. Their fairy princess dressed in pink and reflecting light all around her had joined them. All shared archangel hugs.

"It looks like everyone is ready. Shall we be off?" asked Ariel.

A chorus signaled their agreement. Off they went, waving to the others who had come to investigate and were peering out the porch door.

Ariel turned to Sandalphon and said, "Please continue to play your delightful music while we transport part of the way."

They held hands and found themselves on the roadway leading to the party destination. Fields of four-leaf clovers surrounded them. In the distance, they could see the hills and mounds surrounding the thatched roofs. Tall, stately trees encircled the dance floor. They were almost there. Once Sandalphon's musical notes made their way to the houses and tickled their ears, the quiet neighborhood came alive. The trees shook their leaves and twisted their boughs in welcome. Faces appeared on their tree trunks. Fairies joined them in their colorful outfits flitting this way and that. Leprechauns came tripping out of their dwellings, decked out in green suits with cornered hats covering most of their orange hair. Bottles were raised in a welcome toast. Smoke rings trailed behind them. They ran as fast as they could.

"Top of the Morning! Welcome back!" greeted Paddy. "The tables and chairs are ready, and I can see the fairies have decorated the area with flower garlands. The trees have graced the tables with their apples. I'll be right back with refreshments and our dancing shoes. If you need anything, let me know. Your wish is our command."

The group moved over to the dance floor and table area. They watched the fairies ring the gazebo with garland. Colorful flowers adorned the pillars and tables, welcoming everyone to take a seat.

Paddy and a following marched toward them with an assortment of refreshments. Apple pies were set on the tables to the delight of the apple trees, along with trays of enticing food. Plates and utensils were not forgotten. Paddy's wife and daughter, Caitlin and Colleen, brought up the rear and greeted their guests.

Sandalphon let his music drift off into silence as Archangel Ariel spoke, "Thank you one and all for the food, decorations, and most importantly, your welcome and merriment. Our dear friends have returned from a very long adventure and want to spend some time with you."

"Cheers!" sang out Paddy as he raised his bottle high. Everyone followed suit with shouts of 'cheers' and knee-smacking. Bottles clanked, silverware clanged, and conversation halted so food could be enjoyed. After the dishes were removed, tables cleaned up, and they had relaxed for a wee bit, the leprechauns treated everyone to an exhibition of unusual smoke rings. A competition was soon underway. Their cheers were interrupted when Sandalphon said 'River Dance,' and the group ignited, scurrying to put on their dance shoes and find their places.

Fairies danced in the rafters, trees rustled their leaves, and the observers raucously clapped before the music began. Led by

Sandalphon, the fiddlers started to play when the dance team stepped out in front. The tempo increased, and the dancers hurried to keep up. When it reached its crescendo, the weary collapsed to the ground laughing and giggling.

Those who ventured to get up made their way to the beverages, and soon others followed.

"Time for dessert!" yelled out Caitlin and Coleen. They smiled at each other, winked, and then added, "Apple pie." Tree leaves rustled in approval. There were large plates for the adults, medium-sized for the leprechauns, and tiny button-sized dishes for the fairies. Everyone was lost in thought as they marveled at the deliciousness of the apples in the pie.

After lazing around for a bit, Sandalphon called out once again, "River Dance!"

Everyone jumped up and scurried around, removing plates, putting shoes back on, and finding their favorite spots. The dancing began without delay to the delight of all. They danced and danced and danced some more. The tempo reached a feverish pitch, and then it was over. Exhausted but delighted bodies lined the ground, except for the Archangels who stood watch over the gathering. No one wanted to move.

Ariel asked, "Did everyone have a good time?"

The affirmative moans and groans of exhausted partygoers filled the air. Some had the energy to vocalize a *Yes.*

Ariel continued, "It is time for us to go. Our special guests have completed their last mission and are here to stay, at least for a while. She winked toward Angie, Andrew, Mary, and Matthew, who returned her glance with an astonished look.

Would there be a new adventure in their future? wondered Angie

Paddy started to give his traditional Irish blessing about the road rising up to meet you. They listened, enjoyed the words, and then raised their glasses and bottles in a toast while others gave a thumbs-up sign.

"Thank you all!" responded Angie while the others nodded in agreement. "What Ariel said is true. We completed our mission, and we are living here, so we will come to visit again. And until we meet again, may the angels keep you safe."

They held hands and skipped down the lane to the melody of an Irish jig played cheerfully by Sandalphon. As soon as they were out of sight, they transported the rest of the way. They said goodbyes to Sandalphon and Ariel and enjoyed their comforting archangel hugs. They shuffled to their beds, where they collapsed into a sound sleep.

The next day they planned to go downtown to eat dinner at the gazebo. An early arrival afforded them plenty of time to visit with the trees who surrounded the field. Dinner was a delectable treat followed by delicious ice cream cones. Twilight started to throw shadows, and crowds began to gather. Excited chatter filled the air and then total silence in anticipation of the spectacular light display, thanks to the fireflies.

The tree lighting display went dark as millions of fireflies appeared and performed a synchronized mating show. The males demonstratively flashed their lights and then went dark. The females lit up the area flying in circles, gently flashing their lights. Then they went dark. Once again, the males emphatically flashed their lights. After a brief darkness, the females were back, twirling and swirling while gently flashing their lights. When the trees relit their decorative lightning, it signaled the fireflies' departure for the evening.

Now was as good a time as ever, thought Angie, so she brought up a topic she wanted to discuss, "Did you notice that Ariel said we would be home for a while? I have so many questions."

How long will we be home?

Where will our next adventure take us?

Will we meet more new Archangels?

What will they have dominion over?

What will their talents be?

Will we go back to Tenalp?

Will we revisit Legna's planet?

Will we revisit Hcar and his family?

To find out the answers to all these questions, look for the next book in the series.

Afterward

Bringing you information about the 15 Archangels in *Angel Blessings Believe* and 15 more in *Angel Blessings Imagine*, have resulted in a couple of amazing journeys.

Angie is already anxious for her next adventure and is bugging the author to get writing.

When Archangel Michael and our favorite archangels enlighten us about what they would like to tell you about next, and as we learn which Archangels want to come along, the journey will begin.

It will be fun to see where we will go and what we will do.

Remember, your guardian angels and archangels are always with you. You just have to talk to them. You will be glad you did.

Angel Blessings to all.

Appendix I
Your Guide to the Angels

Your Archangels are standing by waiting for you

Don't pray to angels – Ask and thank them for help or guidance

They are the messengers with a direct line to the Creator

- Take a deep breath in
- Exhale out all negativity
- Repeat 3 times
- Take a fourth deep breath while you make your request
- Send your request to "all archangels" or to specific ones
- Blow your request up toward the angels
- End with: Thank you

Sample: Dear Archangels (or insert specific name) Thank you for helping me with (request)

************Angel Blessings Believe** *********

Archangel Ariel – Pale Pink - Nature

Animals & pets – help the sick & find the lost

Environment – Keep clean & healthy & repair

Provide for the protectors of nature

Gardens & plants to flourish

Landscape – to grow well, thrive, heal

Nature – Helps guide the world to protect

Archangel Azrael – Creamy White - Crossing Over

Death – help cross over

Grief – help heal those left behind so we can move on

Heartache – heal all types of heartache

Archangel Chamuel – Pale Green - Peace

Peace for self, loved ones & the world

Find missing item, career, or loved one

Archangel Gabriel – Copper – Communication

Childbirth, raising, health, and happiness

Parenting

Adoption

Authors and writers

Musicians

Artists

Communication in all forms

Spreading Love

Archangel Haniel – Pale Blue Moonlight - Intuition

Understanding myself and others

Accepting myself as I am

Accepting others for what they are

Accepting my life as the life, I chose

Archangel Jeremiel – Dark Purple – Life Purpose

Understanding life's purpose

Receiving spiritual visions and messages

Understanding divine guidance

Life review

Adjustments to current life's path

Archangel Jophiel – Dark Pink - Beauty

Beautify thoughts

Beautify life

Archangel Metatron – Violet & Green – Time Management

Envision: Merkabah or healing cube moving over your head

Prioritize all aspects of my life and my job

Purify mind, emotions, energy

Watch over children

Child development including spiritual gifts

Career support and guidance as a healer

Archangel Michael – Royal Purple, Royal Blue & Gold - Protection

Protection - homes – keep safe

Protection - possessions – keep safe

Safety

Travel – cars – mine & those around me

Travel – people – me & my occupants & those around me

Divine Purpose – guidance

Peace

Guidance

Equipment repair

Career protection

Reputation protection

Relationships

Lower energies protection

Archangel Raguel – Pale Blue - Harmony

Healing arguments, conflicts, feuds, and misunderstandings

Bringing harmony to situations and relationships

Attracting wonderful new friends

Guidance in a loving, healthy direction

Orderliness, fairness, harmony, and justice

Hope

Relationship between angels and humans

Archangel Raphael – Emerald Green - Healing

Doctor, finding the best

Doctor, quick appointment

Feel comfortable in my body

Feel Good

Good health and well-being

Healing of self, friends, and family

Illness, injuries

Medical career guidance

Medical school guidance

Travel safely

Travel belongings arrive safely and as scheduled

Archangel Raziel – Rainbow – Dreams

Turns knowledge into practical wisdom

Helps humans apply knowledge until it becomes spiritualized and second nature

Help us stay focused

Avoid tempting distractions

Attune to a higher self to connect to divine wisdom

Esoteric wisdom with healing intention

Recordkeeper of ancient wisdom and secrets

Akashic Records

Past life healing and vow clearing and convert those lessons to present-day life

Helps heal from painful memories and traumas so can move forward

Archangel Sandalphon – Turquoise - Music

Prayers – deliver to Heaven

Music, healing

Music, harmonious

Voice

Instruments, music

Archangel Uriel – Yellow - Education

Knowledge

Wisdom

Understanding

Ideas

Insight

Archangel Zadkiel – Deep Indigo Blue - Memory

Helps students remember facts and figures for tests

Helps us choose forgiveness, compassions

Memory

Heal emotional pain and negative memories, anger,

    victimhood

Helps us remember the good experiences and memories

Healer of the mind

**************Angel Blessings Imagin**e ************

Archangel Arariel – Red – Water & stupidity

    Fisherman ask for big catches, good luck, to safely travel the waters and return home

- Ocean, sea or any water travels – keeps safe
- Stupid people – helps avoid making wrong or stupid decisions
- Water – find, clean, provide where need such as rain
- Wash away negativity
- Clear brain fog

Archangel Ariana – Powdery Blue - Children

- Full potential - Recognize and acknowledge in our children
- Crystal healing
- Gain a higher perspective
- Guidance and assistance with special needs and disabled children
- Transition to higher enlightenment

Archangel Barachiel – Green with red rose petals - Blessings, sweetness, lightning, storms

- Storms and lightning – keep everyone and everything safe
- Blessings - for our lives with family and friends, work, etc
- keep us sweet and loving
- Open heart - to break down any protective walls we have built
- Open mind - to hear, acknowledge and consider other's points of view
- Fear of the unknown - release
- Desires - receive including good fortune and abundance
- Laughter & joy - help us with a sense of humor
- Positive outlook
- Good fortune - including gamblers and lottery & bingo players
- Imaginations - sensitivity, inspiration, discernment, thoughtfulness & creative
- Guardian Angels - help us communicate and work with our

Archangel Butyalil – Multi-colored orb – Delicate balance of planets in Cosmos

- Inner earth – calm all disturbances
- Ley Lines - pressure release from within the earth's surface
- Synchronicity - maintain between all living beings throughout the cosmos
- Balance – maintain everywhere
- Awareness – raise

Archangel Christiel – Golden yellow – Peace and Love

- Negativity and confusion - dissolve
- Panic - calm
- Energy - shower us with sun energy
- Protection - shower us with calming mist
- Illuminate - with warmth inside and out
- Hope - never lose and never give up
- Past life cords - dissolve and clear
- Higher outcome – enlighten
- Highest Path – clarify

Archangel Fhelyai – Sunny yellow - Nature, animals and plant life

- Nature calming - heal and protect after a disturbance or catastrophe
- Nature communication: - connect and communicate with animals and pets
- Nature guidance and wisdom - regarding pets, animal and plant kingdoms
- Nature love - send love to all animals and plants everywhere
- Plants - remind to reach down deep into the soil and turn towards the sun
- Veterinarians and shelters - assist those in their care

Archangel Gadiel – Yellow and green - Protection, dilemmas, decisions, empowerment

Imagine - tying your requests to a yellow balloon and let it go into the blowing wind while you call Gabriel three times

- Heart's desire - See what's in my heart in those around me
- Loving path - enter dreams and illuminate loving path
- Guardian angels - Ask them to intervene on my behalf

- Visualize – loving path – with use of reflective mirror
- Dilemma – making good decisions and choices
- Confusion - clear atmosphere
- Caution - change cautious yellow to green go
- Negative feelings – release
- Life's trials and tribulations - rise up from being victim
- Arguments - lovingly resolve
- Disagreements – change to compassion
- Frustrations – change to forgiveness
- Highest good - release anything that does not serve my highest good
- Loving path of abundance and prosperity – lead toward

Archangel Gersisa – Steel grey – Inner earth

- Peace and balance - restore to all planets after a disturbance
- Negative energy - clear within and without our planet
- Solar flares - keep under control
- Moon and her tides - keep under control
- Earthquakes, volcanic eruptions and all negative uneasiness - keep under control
- Ley Lines - keep intact and connected to minimize the earth's outward disturbances

Archangel Manakel – Crystal clear blue – Oceans and Knowledge of Good and Evil

- Aquatic life – protect
- Oceans - achieve balance
- guide the mammals, fish, and sea dwelling plant life to avoid overcrowding
- bring stability, confidence and harmony to all within the oceans and on the lands

- help bring harmony to my emotional, physical, mental and spiritual levels
- Fears and negativity - transform into positivity
- Good from evil – understanding
- Evil - help remove
- Good - help see the good in all and the potential in all
- Dreams, daydreams and intuition – help me understand
- Bad behavior – helps to be a better person and heal bad behavior

Archangel Mariel – Magenta with blue - Truth, Justice, Mercy and Memories

- Soul chakra - clearing to keep open channel to life's purpose
- Memories - keep intact, from this life and from prior lives
- Memories – remove painful memories
- Truth - Stand up for what is right and remember my own truth
- Abilities and gifts - loving use of
- Intuitive guidance – following
- Sense of self – obtain stronger
- Remorse and Dread - Release
- Forgiveness – myself and others
- Love and mercy – fill with

Archangel Nathaniel – Red and Orange – Karma, fire energy, balance, harmony & trust

Reminds us: What we send out, comes back to us Send out good vibrations to get them back Exercise: Imagine lighting a red candle and watch the negativity burn and float away

- Negativity - clear away from my life
- Karma - work with on my karma by nudging in the right direction

- help us if I am part of an advanced group working on a group karma
- bring balance, harmony, and trust into my life and in the lives of those around me
- Balance - restore after significant life changes

Archangel Orion – Midnight blue with Starlight – Cosmos and universe

- Spread a blanket of stars to signal that it was time for sleep
- Peace - help find
- Potential - discover full potential
- Help me slow to a lesser frequency and vibration to I can see the entire picture
- Bigger picture – see every faucet from different perspective and how the pieces fit together and not focus on the small details
- Harmony and balance - help achieve
- Energy clearing - releasing dark and negative energy
- Vibration - open me to receive and understand a higher vibration
- Spiritual gifts – How to open, understand and use
- Channeling – help with hearing from all the archangels
- Manifest – help with dreams, aspirations and inner-wishes

Archangel Phanuel – Blue (& red is evil lurks) - Good & Evil

- Good – find good in everyone
- Negativity - distinguish negativity from evil
- evil – remove from around me and the others that I care about
- Peace and hope - keep in the heart
- Judging - keep from judging others
- Repentance - for actions past and present
- Guilt and regret – help overcome

- Corruption – free world from corrupted leaders and people who don't see good
- Motivation - for change
- Truth versus lies – see difference
- Loving path – stay on
- Good - Help see and desire only the good

Archangel Purlimiek – Blue/green – Nature, harmony and healing

- Nature opportunities - provide more opportunities to be with
- Nature energy - bring forth in person or when looking at picture
- Protection – protect and tend to nature
- Raise the consciousness of those cutting down valuable forests and doing harm
- Bees – keep alive and prospering
- Calm nature - after a negative event
- Nature's treasures - locate, understand and benefit from – Sandalwood, Patchouli, Frankincense, Chamomile, etc

Archangel Selaphiel – Crimson red – Planets and prayer

- Prayer - motivation to express deepest thoughts and feelings
- Planets - Rule the movement
- Exorcisms – preside over
- Music - Bring forth prayerful music and lead the heavenly choir
- Calm - household, community and entire planet, especially after disturbance
- Fears – understand and guide me to help me and others
- People in need - give wisdom and compassion for people in need
- Stress – relief
- Distractions block out

- Addictions – healing
- Dreams – interpret
- Children – protect

Appendix II
Archangel Specialties

Abilities and gifts - loving use of	Mariel
Abundance - guides you toward	Gadiel
Acceptance - self, others for who they are	Haniel
Addiction – healing	Selaphiel
Adoption	Gabriel
Akashic Records	Raziel
Anger - removal	Zadkiel
Animals	Fhelyai
Animals – sick, lost	Ariel
Aquatic life – protect	Manakel
Arguments - heal	Raguel
Arguments - lovingly resolve	Gadiel
Artists - communicate through art	Gabriel
Aspirations - manifest	Orion
Authors	Gabriel
Awareness – raise	Butyalil
Bad behavior - heal, convert to better person	Manakel
Balance - restore after significant life changes	Nathaniel
Balance - help achieve	Orion
Beautify - thoughts	Jophiel

Beautify - life	Jophiel
Beautify - mind	Jophiel
Beauty - all aspects	Jophiel
Bees – keep alive, prospering	Purlimiek
Bigger picture – see every faucet and how fit together	Orion
Blessings - for self, family and friends, work, etc.	Barachiel
Brain fog - clear	Arariel
Calm - all especially after disturbance	Selaphiel
Calm nature - after a negative event	Purlimiek
Career – protection	Michael
Career – find new	Chamuel
Career support - as healer	Metatron
Caution - change cautious yellow to green go	Gadiel
Channeling – hear messages from all the archangels	Orion
Child development - including spiritual gifts	Metatron
Childbirth - raise, health, happiness	Gabriel
Children	Ariana
Children - disabilities - guidance, assistance	Ariana
Children - recognize, acknowledge their full potential	Ariana
Children - special needs - guidance, assistance	Ariana
Children - watch over	Metatron
Children – protect	Selaphiel
Communication - all forms	Gabriel

Compassion	Zadkiel
Conflicts - heal	Raguel
Confusion - clear atmosphere	Gadiel
Corruption – rid world from corrupted leaders and people	Phanuel
Cosmos	Orion
Crossing Over	Azrael
Crystals - use for healing	Ariana
Daydreams - understand	Manakel
Death	Azrael
Decisions	Gadiel
Desires - receive including good fortune, abundance	Barachiel
Different perspective - see bigger picture	Orion
Dilemma – making good decisions, choices	Gadiel
Dilemmas	Gadiel
Disagreements – change to compassion	Gadiel
Distractions - avoid tempting ones	Raziel
Distractions - block out	Selaphiel
Divine guidance - understand	Jeremiel
Divine purpose – guidance	Michael
Divine wisdom - attune, connect	Raziel
Doctor - find best	Raphael
Doctor - quick appointment	Raphael

Dreams	Raziel
Dreams - manifest	Orion
Dreams – interpret	Selaphiel
Earthquakes, all negative uneasiness - keep under control	Gersisa
Education	Uriel
Education - remember facts, figures	Zadkiel
Emotional pain - heal	Zadkiel
Empowerment	Gadiel
Energy - clearing and releasing dark, negative energy	Orion
Energy - shower us with sun energy	Christiel
Enlightenment - transition higher	Ariana
Environment – clean, healthy	Ariel
Equipment - repair	Michael
Esoteric wisdom - healing intention	Raziel
Evil - help remove	Manakel
Evil – remove from self and others that I care about	Phanuel
Exorcisms – preside over	Selaphiel
Fairness	Raguel
Fear of the unknown – release	Barachiel
Fears - ease and transform into positivity	Manakel
Fears – understand and guide to help self and others	Selaphiel
Feel comfortable - in my body	Raphael

Feel good - general feeling of well being	Raphael
Feuds - heal	Raguel
Fire energy	Nathaniel
Fish - help all water dwelling creatures	Manakel
Fisherman - luck, safe travels, return, big catches	Arariel
Focus - retain	Raziel
Forests - raise consciousness of those cutting down, doing harm	Purlimiek
Forgiveness	Zadkiel
Forgiveness – myself, others	Mariel
Frequency - slow down to see entire picture	Orion
Friendship - attract wonderful new ones	Raguel
Frustrations – change to forgiveness, understanding	Gadiel
Gardens - flourish	Ariel
Good - help see, desire only the good	Phanuel
Good - help see the good, potential in all	Manakel
Good – find good in all	Phanuel
Good fortune - everyone and gamblers, lottery, bingo players	Barachiel
Good from evil – understand	Manakel
Good health and well-being	Raphael
Grief - from loss	Azrael
Guardian angels - intervene on my behalf	Gadiel

Guardian Angels - help us communicate, work with our	Barachiel
Guidance	Michael
Guidance - in a loving, healthy direction	Raguel
Guidance - as healer	Metatron
Guilt – overcome	Phanuel
Harmony	Nathaniel
Harmony	Purlimiek
Harmony - to emotional, physical, mental, spiritual levels	Manakel
Harmony - everywhere	Manakel
Harmony - help achieve	Orion
Healing - in general	Purlimiek
Healing - from illness and ailments	Raphael
Healing - self, friends, family	Raphael
Health - good well-being	Raphael
Heart's desire - understand self, those around me	Gadiel
Heartache - from loss	Azrael
Higher outcome – enlighten	Christiel
Higher perspective - achieve	Ariana
Higher self - attune, connect	Raziel
Highest good - release anything that does not serve my highest good	Gadiel
Highest Path – clarify	Christiel

Hope	Raguel
Hope - never lose, never give up	Christiel
Hope - retain	Phanuel
Ideas	Uriel
Illness	Raphael
Illuminate - with warmth inside, out	Christiel
Imaginations - sensitivity, inspiration, discernment, thoughtfulness, creative	Barachiel
Injuries	Raphael
Inner Earth	Gersisa
Inner earth – calm all disturbances	Butyalil
Inner-wishes - manifest	Orion
Insight	Uriel
Instruments	Sandalphon
Intuition	Haniel
Intuition - understand	Manakel
Intuitive guidance – follow	Mariel
Judging - avoid judging others	Phanuel
Justice	Raguel
Justice	Mariel
Karma - work with on my karma by nudging in the right direction	Nathaniel
Knowledge	Uriel

Knowledge - apply until becomes second nature	Raziel
Knowledge - turn into practical wisdom	Raziel
Lands - stability, confidence, harmony to all on land	Manakel
Landscape – grow, thrive, heal	Ariel
Laughter and joy - help us with a sense of humor	Barachiel
Ley Lines - keep intact to minimize the earth's outward disturbances	Gersisa
Ley Lines - pressure release from within the earth's surface	Butyalil
Lies - recognize	Phanuel
Life Purpose - understand, adjust	Jeremiel
Life review	Jeremiel
Life's trials and tribulations - rise up from being victim	Gadiel
Lightening – keep safe	Barachiel
Lost - find missing item	Chamuel
Love	Christiel
Love – spread	Gabriel
Love and mercy – fill with	Mariel
Loved one – find	Chamuel
Loving path – lead toward	Gadiel
Loving path - fill dreams with knowledge	Gadiel
Loving path - illuminate	Gadiel
Loving path – stay on	Phanuel

Mammals - help	Manakel
Medical career - guidance	Raphael
Memories	Mariel
Memories - heal from painful ones	Raziel
Memories - keep intact from this life and from prior lives	Mariel
Memories – remove painful memories	Mariel
Memory	Zadkiel
Memory - heal from the bad	Zadkiel
Memory - remember the good	Zadkiel
Mercy	Mariel
Messages - receive spiritual	Jeremiel
Mind – help with	Zadkiel
Misunderstandings - heal	Raguel
Moon and her tides - keep under control	Gersisa
Motivation - for change	Phanuel
Music - all forms	Sandalphon
Music - harmonious	Sandalphon
Music - to heal	Sandalphon
Music - prayerful & heavenly	Selaphiel
Musicians - communicate through music	Gabriel
Nature - protection world-wide	Ariel
Nature calming - heal, protect after a disturbance or	Fhelyai

catastrophe

Nature communication - connect, communicate with animals, pets	Fhelyai
Nature energy - bring forth	Purlimiek
Nature guidance and wisdom - for pets, animal, plant kingdoms	Fhelyai
Nature love - send love to all animals and plants everywhere	Fhelyai
Nature opportunities - provide more opportunities to be with	Purlimiek
Nature's treasures - locate, understand, benefit from	Purlimiek
Negative energy - clear within and without our planet	Gersisa
Negative feelings – release	Gadiel
Negativity - clear away from my life	Nathaniel
Negativity - distinguish from evil	Phanuel
Negativity - removal	Zadkiel
Negativity - transform to positivity	Manakel
Negativity – wash away	Arariel
Negativity and confusion – dissolve	Christiel
Oceans - achieve balance	Manakel
Oceans - stability, confidence, harmony to all on oceans	Manakel
Oils, natural - understand, use	Purlimiek
Open heart - to break down walls we have built	Barachiel

Open mind - to hear, acknowledge, consider other viewpoints	Barachiel
Orderliness	Raguel
Panic – calm	Christiel
Parenting	Gabriel
Past life - heal, clear, convert lessons to present-day life	Raziel
Past life cords - dissolve and clear	Christiel
Peace	Chamuel
Peace	Michael
Peace	Christiel
Peace - find	Orion
Peace - keep in the heart	Phanuel
Peace and balance - restore to all planets after a disturbance	Gersisa
People in need - give wisdom, compassion	Selaphiel
Perspective - see bigger picture	Orion
Pets – sick, lost	Ariel
Planets - balance	Butyalil
Planets - rule movement	Selaphiel
Plants - guide roots down deep into the soil and turn towards the sun	Fhelyai
Plants - flourish	Ariel
Positive outlook	Barachiel

Potential - discover full potential	Orion
Prayer - motivation to express deepest thoughts, feelings	Selaphiel
Prayers – deliver to Heaven	Sandalphon
Prioritize - all aspects of life and job	Metatron
Prosperity - lead down the loving path toward	Gadiel
Protection	Gadiel
Protection - possessions – keep safe	Michael
Protection - homes – keep safe	Michael
Protection - of everything, everyone	Michael
Protection - shower us with calming mist	Christiel
Protection – protect, tend to nature	Purlimiek
Protection - from lower energies	Michael
Purify - mind, emotions, energy	Metatron
Regret - help overcome	Phanuel
Relationships	Michael
Relationships - between angels and humans	Raguel
Relationships -bring harmony	Raguel
Remorse and dread – Release	Mariel
Repentance - for actions past, present	Phanuel
Reputation - protection	Michael
Safety	Michael
Sea Dwelling creatures, plants - help	Manakel

Sense of self – obtain stronger	Mariel
Solar flares - keep under control	Gersisa
Soul chakra - clear to keep open channel to life's purpose	Mariel
Soulmate - find	Chamuel
Spiritual gifts – understand, use	Orion
Stars - tend to	Orion
Storms – keep safe from	Barachiel
Stress – relief	Selaphiel
Stupid people – help avoid wrong or stupid decisions	Arariel
Sweetness - keep us sweet, loving	Barachiel
Synchronicity - maintain balance throughout the cosmos	Butyalil
Time Management	Metatron
Traumas - heal	Raziel
Travel - belongings arrive safely, on time	Raphael
Travel - safety	Raphael
Travel – cars – protect me, those around me	Michael
Travel – people – protect me, those around me	Michael
Trust - self, others	Nathaniel
Truth	Mariel
Truth - stand up for what is right, remember my own truth	Mariel
Truth versus lies – see difference	Phanuel

Understand - self, others	Haniel
Understanding	Uriel
Universe	Orion
Veterinarians and shelters - assist those in their care	Fhelyai
Vibration - receive, understand a higher vibration	Orion
Vibration - slow down to see entire picture	Orion
Visions - receive spiritual	Jeremiel
Visualize – loving path – with use of reflective mirror	Gadiel
Voice	Sandalphon
Volcanic eruptions, all negative uneasiness - keep under control	Gersisa
Water – find, clean, provide where need such as rain	Arariel
Water travels - keeps safe	Arariel
Wisdom, ancient - recordkeeper including secrets	Raziel
Wisdom	Raziel
Wisdom	Uriel
Writers	Gabriel

About the Author

Her first book, *Angel Blessings Believe,* relayed many of Patty's personal experiences. However, we are happy to report that Patty is alive and well. The incidents in chapter 3, "Signs Received," are true and are some of the many signs Patty has received over the years. If you look back on the twists and turns of your life, you may find signs too. There is no such thing as coincidence. It was necessary to have Angie pass over to be able to introduce you to the archangels.

In *Angel Blessings Imagine*, Patty introduces you to 15 different Archangels, and her main character, Angie, takes you on quite a few amazing adventures.

Communication has always been Patty's forte, and her love of people has led to her many successes. She has always listened to the inner voice that wakes her up in the morning and guides her through her day. She rarely remembers her dreams. Instead, she wakes up to a gentle command. She thought it was her inner voice that had worked out situations in her dream state, but that theory changed when the voice told her to write a book. She let her imagination run wild, and she wrote many short stories that later became chapters in her books.

She calls on Archangel Michael to keep her family safe and Archangel Raphael to keep them all healthy. She receives daily, author-related guidance from Archangel Gabriel.

One morning, she woke up to the vision of a book cover. She started to google the components, and in no time at all, she was miraculously guided to the artist and the exact vision she had received. From then on, there was no doubt she was receiving archangel guidance to tell their story.

She learned meditation, something she had tried in the 1970s, but she could never calm her mind down and ended up disliking it while her husband has continued meditating to this day. Under the expert guidance of davidji through an online course, she learned to rely on meditation as a necessary preparation for her daily writing sessions. Before she starts writing, she follows the guidance of Mike Dooley and is heard yelling "Wahoo!" after meditating to get in an upbeat mood. It works.

She was guided to have her husband of forty-plus years help her create the ultimate loving worlds. Her mom, who entered the spirit world several years ago, had been her editor through life and had encouraged her to take typing and shorthand during her school years. Over the years, she helped her with spelling, grammar, and editing her rewrites; she has been by her side through this journey as her spirit guide. They have the same name and are kindred spirits. Not only is her presence felt, but also, her birthday shows up on the clock continually, as does Patty's birth date.

Watch for the next book in the series in which Angie continues her mission for world peace through love.

CPSIA information can be obtained
at www.ICGtesting.com
Printed in the USA
BVHW070051010921
615653BV00001B/38